"You're not quite what you seem, are you?"

At Rees's words, Julia's heart leapt into her throat. Surely he hadn't guessed. "I'm not?" she managed.

"No," he said. "You were recommended as a highly capable personal assistant, so you can't be the innocent you pretend."

"By innocent I suppose you mean virginal?"

Rees looked nonplussed. "Well . . . yes."

"That's stupid," she said. "Why can't a successful career woman also remain a virgin?"

"I suppose she could if she weren't a beautiful sexy girl like you. I don't believe I'm the first man to ever lust after you."

Julia thought that was pretty straight talking. She said, "I need to be in love. I'm not interested in casual sex."

"Nor am I," Rees said. "But I know what I want."

ROBERTA LEIGH wrote her first book at the age of nineteen and since then has written more than seventy romance novels, as well as many books and film series for children. She has also been an editor of a woman's magazine, but writing romance fiction remains one of her greatest joys. She lives in Hampstead, London, and has one son.

Books by Roberta Leigh

LOVE MATCH

HARLEQUIN PRESENTS

169—CUPBOARD LOVE
175—MAN WITHOUT A HEART
182—UNWILLING BRIDEGROOM
193—TOO YOUNG TO LOVE
204—GIRL FOR A MILLIONAIRE
233—NOT A MARRYING MAN
461—CONFIRMED BACHELOR
819—NO TIME FOR MARRIAGE
954—MAID TO MEASURE
1026—A RACY AFFAIR
1043—TOO BAD TO BE TRUE
1066—AN IMPOSSIBLE MAN TO LOVE
1092—NO MAN'S MISTRESS
1115—STORM CLOUD MARRIAGE

HARLEQUIN ROMANCE

1196—DARK INHERITANCE
1269—PRETENCE
1424—THE VENGEFUL HEART
1696—MY HEART'S A DANCER
1715—IN NAME ONLY
1783—CINDERELLA IN MINK
1800—SHADE OF THE PALMS
1893—IF DREAMS CAME TRUE

ROBERTA LEIGH

not without love

Harlequin Books

TORONTO • NEW YORK • LONDON
AMSTERDAM • PARIS • SYDNEY • HAMBURG
STOCKHOLM • ATHENS • TOKYO • MILAN

Harlequin Presents first edition November 1989
ISBN 0-373-11217-3

Original hardcover edition published in 1989
by Mills & Boon Limited

Printed in U.S.A.

CHAPTER ONE

REES DENTON banged his fist on the boardroom table. 'I don't need a bodyguard and I won't have one. Never! Is that understood?'

'Understood but not agreed,' said Sir Andrew Seymour, chairman of Engineering 2000, and the other directors around the table murmured their agreement. 'Be sensible, Rees. You can't ignore these threats on your life.'

'Whoever made them is a crank,' Rees said irritably.

'Cranks are the ones to watch out for,' put in a balding man with glasses. 'History shows——'

'I don't give a damn what history shows!' Rees cut in, his dark eyebrows drawn into a frown. 'The police can handle it.'

'They are,' Sir Andrew intervened. 'But they need more time. They're working through the passenger list and checking all next of kin. But whittling down the suspects takes time, and this crank, as you call him, could strike any moment.'

'I fail to see how a bodyguard will help,' Rees said obstinately, smoothing back his thick black hair with a strong, well-manicured hand.

'They are specially trained for this kind of work,' another director explained.

Rees reflected on this, then shook his head. 'No, I won't have my every move monitored. I'd feel like a kid with a nanny.'

Resigned glances were exchanged and throats cleared.

'Be sensible, Rees,' Sir Andrew reiterated. 'It's your life we're talking about. The man's dangerous.'

The chorus of endorsements was louder than before. This threat to the life of their managing director had them worried, coming as it did so soon after the crash of the plane which had only just been fitted with Engineering 2000's special 'grey box', devised by Rees to make flying safer.

Most people in the situation in which he now found himself would have immediately agreed to protection. But Rees Denton wasn't 'most people'. Not only was he a brilliant inventor, organiser and negotiator—invaluable assets to the company—but, like most individualists, he was also obstinate.

He stood up, all six foot two of determined muscle and grace, and scanned his fellow directors with piercing dark eyes. 'No guard,' he reiterated. 'That's my last word on the subject. Now, I suggest we get down to the business of the day and waste no more time.'

For the next hour the meeting continued, and as soon as it was over Rees departed, giving pressure of work as his reason for not lunching with the board, though the directors knew quite well that he merely wished to avoid further discussion on a subject he had declared *verboten*.

'We can't let him get away with it,' the vice-chairman stated. 'If anything happened to him . . .'

'He's not a man you can order around,' Sir Andrew said. 'But you're right. We have to do something.'

'What do you propose?'

'I'm not sure.' Sir Andrew's voice was as smooth as the silver-grey hair brushed back from his high forehead, which gave him the look of a professor rather than that of the astute City man he was.

But Sir Andrew was very sure indeed, for he had known the fuss Rees would make, and had allowed for it, determined to get his own way by stealth if necessary.

As soon as lunch was over, he went to his office and put in a call to Murray Guardian of Guardian Security, who had been recommended to him by a senior police officer at Scotland Yard. A brief word explaining the urgency of the situation, brought him an appointment to see Murray Guardian within the hour, after which, well pleased with himself, he ordered the chauffeur to bring round his car.

Julia Winterton put down the receiver and breathed a sigh of relief. Murray had agreed to see her at four, and if she was lucky he would have another assignment for her. But no more acting nursemaid to the rich and spoilt. She had made it quite clear that, if Guardians couldn't give her the kind of job for which she had been trained, she would leave. But she wanted to give Murray another chance first. Not only was it the ethical thing to do, but she hoped she could twist his arm!

She looked at her watch. It was too early to leave, but she would rather sit at Murray's for the next hour than twiddle her thumbs here. With a cursory glance in the mirror, she left her Sloane Street apartment and took the elevator down to the plush foyer—a tall, willowy girl with long, blue-black hair, and a Miss World body.

Twenty minutes later she was waiting in Murray's reception-room, a smile on her beautifully curved mouth as she remembered how nervously she had waited to see him on that first occasion six months ago, knowing that female security guards were still a rarity, and hoping he wouldn't dismiss her out of hand because she was a model.

But modelling had bored her once she had reached the top, and though the money was fantastic, and her ego massaged every time she walked down the street and someone recognised her from the front cover of Harpers, Tatler or Vogue, she had eventually begun questioning whether the constant battling against sex-hungry males who considered models easy game was worth it all.

It had been a suave City type who had been the last straw. A gentleman during dinner and dancing at Annabel's, he had become a sex-mad octopus outside her front door.

'Bloody hell!' he had exclaimed, when she had levelled him to the ground with a karate chop. 'Where did you learn *that*?'

'I have four brothers,' she had said nonchalantly. 'And they thought I should know how to protect myself!'

He had departed fast, and, though the incident had been amusing in retrospect, it had reinforced her dissatisfaction with her present life. Women were still the butt of sexual innuendo and harassment, no matter what they did, but some professions were more vulnerable to it than others, and show business and modelling were two of them. But what else could she do, and where would she find a man interested in her as a person and not primarily as a bedworthy partner?

After careful deliberation, she concluded that the first thing to do was to change her occupation. The very next day she had read an article in *The Times* about security guards, and had known instantly that this was the work she wanted to do. Careful enquiry told her that the best company was Guardian Security, and within two months of seeing them she had become a fully trained member.

Her hope that a different career would bring romance into her life had not materialised, for apart from Murray

Guardian himself, who oddly she couldn't think of romantically—though he fitted the bill more than any man she knew—there had been no one. But there was still the challenge of the job. If only Murray would *give* her a challenge instead of asking her to act as nanny to a host of ludicrous people. Like the oil baron's son she had escorted from his home in Texas to Eton, his new school in England.

Concordeing across the Atlantic to Dallas, the man next to her had wasted no time putting a pudgy hand on her arm.

'Going on vacation?' he had asked.

'No. I'm on a job. I'm a bodyguard.'

He chuckled. 'Whose body you guarding?'

'Mine.'

'I'd guard it better if you'd let me.'

'I doubt it. I'm a gold medallist in the martial arts.'

That had quickly put paid to *him*, and after seeing gum-chewing Henry Hackenburg Junior safely ensconced in school she had been sent to watch over a sheika, in London for the summer, and seemingly intent on buying out Harrods. Carrying her parcels, her jewellery and her money—no cheques, all cash—Julia had thought long and hard about resigning, for which reason she was now waiting to see Murray.

If he didn't utilise the expensive training he had given her, she would apply to one of his rivals, and if they offered her similar tame assignments she would return to modelling. Yet, even as she said this to herself, she knew she could never go back to the fashion world. Indeed, if it hadn't been for Chris she would never have entered it. Funny, she hadn't thought of him in years.

Blond, blue-eyed Chris, friend of her oldest brother, who had spent most weekends on their estate, and endeared himself to her family by being as fanatic about fitness as they were.

Though she was the only girl among four brothers, she had not been spoilt. On the contrary, they had expected her to join them in all their sporting activities. She had enjoyed being 'one of the boys' until she had fallen in love with Chris, but the day he called her 'kiddo'—which happened to be her eighteenth birthday—she had known it was time to change her image. After all, what was the point having wide-spaced violet eyes and silky black hair if the man you were crazy about saw you as 'kiddo'?

A heart-to-heart talk with her mother resulted in her being sent to London for a three-month beauty and modelling course, and her decision to actually become a model had been met with stoical acceptance by her parents.

Her meteoric rise had astonished even herself, though by this time Chris had married and gone abroad, and she was hard put to it to remember she had ever had a crush on him.

The sound of Murray's door opening brought Julia back to the present, and she looked up as he emerged with a tall, distinguished-looking man in his late fifties. Watching them talking in low voices at the door, Julia remembered how nervous she had been the first time she had met Murray Guardian.

'Miss Winterton?' He had come forward to greet her as she had entered his office, and she had instantly liked him. Average in height, this strongly built man in his mid-thirties, with his dark gold hair and piercing blue eyes, had exactly epitomised her idea of someone who owned and ran a security company.

He had waved her to a chair and sat down at his desk which, like its owner, lacked pretension, as did the rest of the furniture in the room, being dark oak and functional.

She had felt comfortable sitting opposite him, for, though his look had been appraising, it had also been respectful. He had clearly been intrigued that someone looking like a model—she hadn't yet told him she was—should want to become a bodyguard.

'Tell me about yourself,' he had said, leaning back in his chair.

'I've been modelling for nearly four years, and want a change.'

His eyebrows had risen. 'It would certainly be *that*.'

'I know.'

'The training's tough, and I fail thirty per cent.'

'You're not putting me off, Mr Guardian. I grew up with four tough brothers who treated me like a fifth!'

'Then there should be no problem.' He smiled. 'How old are you?'

'Twenty-three.'

'Exactly the right age. Store detectives are in great demand.'

She remembered how aghast she had been. 'Store detectives? But I thought I'd——'

'Guard someone from a terrorist attack?'

'Well, yes—no, not exactly.' But she hadn't expected to peer around dress rails in department stores either!

'Take it or leave it,' he had said crisply. 'I've plenty of other candidates.'

Realising she had expected too much, she had capitulated. Once she had proved herself, she could be demanding. Till then, she would keep her mouth shut!

'I'd like to train,' she had said firmly.

'Good. Report here Monday, eight-thirty, with your suitcase. You'll be spending the next six weeks at my country house in Sussex. Good luck.'

It had all sounded so cut and dried, but then security work couldn't afford any beating around the bush. It required nerve, courage, and physical stamina. All of which she had in plenty.

There had been fourteen of them on the course, thirteen men and she the only girl. Murray's country house was a rambling old place set in ten acres, and at times it seemed as if they crawled over every one of them! Still, they were a fit lot, having been hand-picked, a fact that Murray never let them forget as he put them through a gruelling course in self-defence, attack, and undercover work.

Unbelievably, Julia graduated top of her class, and the amused glint in Murray's eyes when he had told her had made her more determined than ever not to be assigned 'female-type' jobs once she had some experience under her belt.

Murray had thrown a party for them that evening in the large oak-beamed reception-room, and she had worn the one dress she had brought with her for this occasion—a violet silk to match her eyes—and let her long, silky hair flow down her back in an ebony swathe.

Every head had turned at her entrance, and it had been *her* turn to be amused. Men were still men, she had thought, and a pretty woman still a target.

Next day Murray had called them in separately.

'Much as I'd like to give you the kind of assignment you want,' he had said to her without preamble, 'I can't.'

'You mean you were serious about my working in a department store?'

'Yes. You deserve better, but many of our jobs require muscle, and even those that don't invariably state they want men.'

'That's discriminatory and against the law,' she had protested.

'I know. So they don't put the request in writing. But if I send a woman, I won't get the work.'

Accepting this, Julia took what was offered, and for six months fumed and fretted her way through a variety of tedious assignments—Henry Hackenburg and the sheika among them—until she had finally had enough.

Hence her coming here today to have a showdown with Murray.

Almost as if he sensed it, he gave her a warm smile and paused in front of her to introduce her to the man beside him. 'Meet my star pupil,' he said. 'Julia, Sir Andrew Seymour. She's the only person on any of my courses who graduated with a hundred per cent pass.'

'Well done.' Sir Andrew was plainly astonished, and gave her such an appraising look that Julia was startled. And at his age, too!

'Wait for me in my office, Julia,' Murray said. 'I'll be with you in a moment.'

Julia did as she was bid. Now that confrontation was imminent, was she prepared to go to another agency if Murray didn't give her what she wanted? Before she could decide, he had returned and perched on the side of his desk.

'Out with it.' He smiled. 'You've something on your mind, haven't you?'

She nodded and told him, and though he appreciated her views, as he always did, he was unable to offer a solution. 'I'm always putting your name forward,' he said, 'but in the final event, it's the clients who make the choice.'

'Then you should start re-educating your clients!'

'Do you have another job *I* can do?' Murray asked, mouth curving. 'If I do as you suggest, I sure as hell won't be able to carry on here!'

'President Reagan's guarded by women as well as men,' Julia asserted.

'I deliver what I'm asked for,' Murray reiterated. 'I——' He was interrupted by the telephone, spoke into it, then glanced at Julia. 'Sir Andrew wants to see me again. Hang on, will you?'

He strode away, returning a few moments later with Sir Andrew.

'My meeting you was extremely fortuitous, Miss Winterton,' Sir Andrew began, and Julia, though she smiled politely, inwardly fumed. If he wanted her to watch over his wife or grandchild, the answer would be no! Didn't Murray ever learn?

But what Sir Andrew wanted of her had nothing to do with his family, and as she heard of the death threats his managing director was receiving her hopes started to rise. Yet there was one question she had to ask, even though she knew it was hardly a tactful one.

'*Was* Mr Denton's invention in any way to blame for the crash?'

'Absolutely not.' Sir Andrew spoke from total conviction. 'It may not make flying a hundred per cent foolproof, but it goes a long way towards it. Forgive me if I don't go into the technical details, but——'

'There's no need,' Murray put in, giving Julia a hard look. 'Sir Andrew wants you to guard Mr Denton until the police discover who's behind these threats.'

'Unfortunately Rees won't accept police protection—won't accept *any* protection, in fact.'

'Why not?' Julia asked.

'He says it will curtail his freedom.'

'What we suggest,' Murray said, pretending not to notice Julia's astonishment, 'is that we guard him without his knowing it.'

Julia's beautifully arched eyebrows rose. 'How?'

'We'll arrange that you stand in for Mrs Williamson, his personal assistant,' Sir Andrew answered before Murray could. 'She's been with Rees for years and is very worried for him—as we all are. We'll get her to say she has to go to Canada to see her mother who is very ill. Rees won't suspect anything because he knows the woman recently had an operation.'

'You seem to have worked things out very well.' Julia smiled. 'But it will only give me a legitimate reason for being with him during the day. What about the evenings?'

'He works late,' Sir Andrew replied.

'And when he doesn't work late, and weekends? What then?'

Both men looked flummoxed, though it was Murray whose brow cleared first. 'You'll have to charm him, Julia; make him so besotted over you that he won't want you out of his sight.'

Sir Andrew chuckled. 'That shouldn't be difficult, if you don't mind my saying so, Miss Winterton. Rees has an eye for the ladies, and you're extremely eye-catching.'

Julia wasn't sure she liked where this might lead. In fact, she was darned sure she didn't! And she wanted to get her position quite clear before deciding whether or not to accept the job.

'Even if Mr Denton finds me attractive, I can't see him wanting to date me all of his spare time.'

'I don't see why not,' Sir Andrew said jovially. 'Rees is very single-minded, and when he sets his sights on a lady, he—well, he's rather inclined to pursue them.'

'And catch them, I suppose?'

Only then did the two men see where Julia's questions were leading, and though Murray couldn't hide a grin, Sir Andrew looked distinctly uncomfortable.

'My dear Miss Winterton, I wasn't suggesting... Believe me, nothing was further from my mind.'

'I'm sure not,' Julia replied evenly, 'but it's very much in mine. I like the sound of this job, Sir Andrew, but there's a limit to what I'm prepared to do in order to get it.'

'Oh, come on, Julia,' Murray said. 'You held your own in the modelling world, so I'm sure you can hold it with Mr Denton.'

Julia was sure too, but she resented having to use her femininity in order to get this assignment. Anyway, what sort of man was Rees Denton? Only an idiot would discount the threats he had been getting. He sounded macho to the point of stupidity—probably considered it a sign of weakness to worry about his safety.

'Come on,' Murray urged again. 'Mata Hari had no trouble, and I can't see you having any either!'

Julia smiled at Murray's confidence in her, though her resentment remained. But she had asked for a challenge, and Rees Denton certainly presented one.

'When do I start?' she asked.

'Tomorrow,' Sir Andrew answered. 'Rees is shut away in his laboratory today and most of tomorrow, which will give me a chance to speak to Mrs Williamson and brief her. I'll get her to say you're the daughter of a friend of hers, and insist you're just the person to take over from her while she's away.'

'But I've never worked in an office in my life!'

'Mrs Williamson won't leave for a couple of days. That should give you plenty of time to learn the ropes.'

Wow! Julia thought. Two whole days to learn to be a personal assistant. Next, he might suggest she study for three and start running the company! Maybe she should tell Murray she had been joking when she had said she was tired of oil barons' sons and child tennis stars! Except Murray wouldn't appreciate the joke.

'Everything settled, then?' he asked, as if guessing her thoughts.

'Yes,' she mumbled.

'Then I'll tell Mrs Williamson to expect you at four tomorrow,' Sir Andrew stated. 'If anything bothers you at any time, don't hesitate to come and talk to me.'

'It's better if Julia talks to *me*,' Murray put in. 'Mr Denton might suspect something if he sees you and Julia in cahoots.'

'Quite right. I hadn't thought of that.'

Knowing the interview was at an end and that Murray would want to get down to the financial aspect, Julia said goodbye and went to the door. She felt Sir Andrew's eyes on her, and knew he was still assessing her, wondering if she could handle Mr Denton—which Murray was probably wondering too. But she'd show them both. Not wishing Rees Denton any harm, she hoped she would have a chance to use her training, for it would be marvellous to prove to Murray once and for all that she was as good as any man—if not better!

An hour later she was back in her apartment, looking through her clothes and trying to decide what to wear for her meeting with her new boss. One thing about modelling—it had given her a sense of style, but whether hers would be suitable for attracting the roving eye of Mr Denton was another matter.

Her hand stopped at a mauve silk Armani suit and, taking it out, she held it against her and looked in the mirror. Thick-fringed violet eyes stared back at her, and lowering them seductively she lifted her long, raven tresses atop her head and pouted her lips—*à la* Mata Hari. But this was the eighties, and an office *femme fatale* wouldn't be so obvious. Maybe she should start off with a bun and heavy spectacles, and gradually graduate to the temptress. But that would take time, and Rees Denton could be lying in a pool of blood by then!

Maybe she'd just be herself. After all, she had never had any trouble attracting men in the past, and Mr Denton, obstinate and foolhardy though he was, was still a man!

Padding into the bathroom, she slipped off her clothes and turned on the shower, enjoying the feel of the cool water needling her skin and forming rivulets between her creamy breasts and down the length of her willowy frame. Her long raven hair wound itself around her shoulders like a swathe, and she pulled it back and plaited it quickly before soaping herself.

What sort of man was her new client? she wondered again. From what Sir Andrew had let drop, he was pig-headed and macho, both of them characteristics she could do without. Still, she must not start off prejudiced, for as Murray had so frequently said during her training: 'Many of the people whose safety we protect may not be the kind we would choose as friends, but we're there to guard them, not judge them, so never, ever allow your emotions to become involved.'

Unhappily, this dictum didn't apply here, Julia admitted as she turned off the shower and wrapped herself in a pink towelling robe. She *had* to form a judgement of Mr Denton in order to make herself attractive to him, as well as to enable her to keep him at arm's length. No easy task, come to think of it, to blow hot one minute and cool the next.

Stop thinking of it, she admonished her reflection as she dressed for a dinner date with a girlfriend. Tomorrow was only a few hours away, and before jumping to any further conclusions about her charge she must first meet him. Only then could she map out a plan to lure him into her net and, if necessary, render him harmless!

CHAPTER TWO

PROMPTLY at four next day Julia arrived at the ten-storey bronze and steel structure in Docklands that housed Engineering 2000.

The interior was equally sparkling, and, as she walked across the white travertine marble floor to the mahogany reception desk in the middle of it, her eyes were drawn to the bank of wall-climbing elevators.

Hardly had she given her name when she was directed to Elevator Three and instructed to go to Room Fifty on the tenth floor. This turned out to be an elegantly furnished office, supervised by an equally elegant Mrs Williamson, a forty-year-old woman who was the epitome of the perfect personal assistant. Julia's confidence plummeted as she wondered how she could possibly follow in such footsteps. Bearing in mind Mrs Williamson was supposed to have personally recommended her to Mr Denton, he would expect her to be pretty damn good. Some hope, when she had never worked in an office in her life!

'I can't tell you how relieved we are to have you,' Mrs Williamson murmured. 'I'm only sorry you have to be here under false pretences.'

'So am I,' Julia said. 'But I've handled far more tricky situations.' Surreptitiously she crossed her fingers.

'You shouldn't find your work here too difficult,' Mrs Williamson went on, assessing her frankly. 'Basically you'll be attending to the more mundane matters, so Mr Denton can concentrate on the important ones.'

'Mundane matters?' Julia questioned.

'Such as keeping tabs on his meetings and appointments, holding the media off his back, dealing with as much of his mail as you can without bothering him... You'll soon pick it up.'

'Oh, sure,' Julia said with bravura, not sure at all. And there was still the matter of making him fall for her and holding him off at one and the same time!

'Mr Denton often works late,' Mrs Williamson continued. 'Which means you often stay behind with him. But that should fit in very well with why you're here,' she said with a conspiratorial smile, before rising and going to the adjoining door. There was a quiet exchange of words as she put her head around it, then she turned and beckoned to Julia. 'Mr Denton will see you now.'

Nervous as a schoolgirl being summoned to the head, Julia walked into the managing director's office. Except no managing director—outside of a Hollywood romantic epic—ever looked like this, she thought, as a six-foot, dark-eyed Adonis, with strong, patrician features and thick ebony hair, came towards her with panther's grace, an easy smile and hand outstretched.

'Sit down and tell me about yourself.' His voice was deep and resonant, his gesture spare as he waved her to a chair and sat opposite her.

Julia's nervousness increased. She had met many good-looking men in the course of her career, but never one quite so handsome and charismatic. She knew he was waiting for her to speak and could have kicked herself for not finding out what Mrs Williamson had told him about her. She could hardly give herself a false curriculum vitae and find it differed drastically from what he had heard.

'Well?' he asked abruptly, his deep-set, dark eyes narrowing as they regarded her.

'I'm the daughter of a friend of your personal assistant,' she said in a rush.

'So I believe.' He leaned back in his chair, still keeping his eyes on her. 'I understand you haven't done this kind of work before, but as you've come with Mrs Williamson's recommendation, that's good enough for me.'

'It's really a matter of common sense, I think,' Julia murmured, feeling her way.

'Not quite. You need to know the names of the people I'm always available to, and the ones I avoid like the plague.'

'I'm sure Mrs Williamson has a list for me,' Julia said easily, 'and I've a good memory.'

He eyed her keenly. 'You don't look a fool,' he said. 'In fact, you look good enough to be a model.'

He meant it as a compliment, she knew, but it wasn't one she appreciated, having deliberately changed her career in order *not* to be judged on her looks. Drat the man! Why was he staring at her like this? Anyone would think he was taking an inventory of her! As his eyes continued roaming over her face and body, she was hard put not to disclose her true identity and see *his* face!

'Don't you like my saying you look like a model?' he asked, correctly reading her irritated expression.

'It's simply that I consider them witless,' she shrugged. 'I mean, how intelligent do you have to be to pose in front of a camera or mince down a catwalk?'

'Not intelligent at all,' he agreed, so readily that she longed to hit him.

'Do you know many, Mr Denton?' The instant she asked the question, she regretted it, for it was too personal coming from someone being interviewed for a job.

'A fair number,' he replied, and gave her such a devastating smile that she regretted he was a client. But he was and, bearing in mind Murray's rule, she would do well to remember it. Except that it was her duty to entice him, a duty that seemed less onerous by the minute.

'You're from London?' he asked.

'Yes. But with Cornish grandparents.'

'Same here. My great-great-grandfather was Spanish, though. Came over as a smuggler, fell in love with an innkeeper's daughter and turned honest!'

Julia laughed. She had wondered about those Latin looks of his, for in all else he seemed decidedly English. Eton and Oxford, she guessed.

'You'll have to do a fair amount of overtime,' he went on. 'I frequently work late and expect you to stay.'

'I don't take shorthand,' she said quickly.

'I rarely give it. My letters are too technical even for an above average secretary. So I use the dictaphone, which gives Mrs Williamson time to use her dictionary!'

Julia hoped he wouldn't ask if she could type, for though she had taken a computer course—during a three-month spell at the beginning of her career when work had been slow—she had subsequently not had time to use it.

'Do you have a boyfriend?'

His question startled her and, aware of it, Rees Denton's wide shoulders lifted. 'No ulterior motive, Miss Winterton, simply that if you stay late, I don't want irate young men barging in to see you. Most of the work I do here is highly confidential.'

'Here?' she echoed, looking around his sumptuously furnished office, with its silver-grey carpet, teak desk and black leather chairs.

'Yes, here,' he replied, and, pressing a button on his desk, enjoyed her amazement as the wall to his left slid back to reveal a drawing office, small, but elaborately equipped.

'How clever,' she murmured.

'Not really.' His smile drew attention to his beautifully shaped, sensuous mouth. 'It's simply that I've an aversion to clutter. I like everything in its place, where I need it, when I need it.'

Julia wondered if that applied to his women too, and had the feeling that the female of the species was needed only in his bed. He was too assertive, too sure of himself to need them anywhere else.

She saw him glance at his watch, and she rose.

'Sorry to rush you,' he apologised. 'But I've a date this evening and have a lot of work to get through.'

Even as she reached the door he was engrossed in a file on his desk. Somewhat disconcerted at how quickly he could refocus his attention, she went into the outer office.

'How did it go?' Mrs Williamson enquired.

'I just about passed. I shouldn't think he suffers fools gladly.'

'Only the ones he's dating,' the older woman smiled.

Julia instantly had an impression of lovely dumb-bells falling like nine-pins around him, and though it irritated her, she knew his susceptibility could make her task here that much easier.

She was still mulling this over when she returned to her apartment, and as she closed the front door the telephone rang. Wondering if it was Mr Denton to say he had changed his mind and didn't want to engage her, she reached to answer it.

'Julia, this is Chris.'

For a split second she couldn't place the whimsical voice, then all at once she did, and couldn't keep the astonishment out of hers as she repeated his name. 'Chris? I don't believe it. Where have you sprung from?'

'I'll tell you when we meet. I hope it can be soon? I saw some fashion photographs of you in a magazine last year and was very impressed.'

'A lot's happened to me since then,' she said. 'But I'd love to see you. Do the boys know you're back in England?'

'I spoke to Rob an hour ago—that's how I got your number.'

Julia was surprised, and with a premonition of the answer that was to come, said, 'How's your wife?'

'Fine, I think. We divorced six months ago.'

'And you suddenly remembered a scrawny girl with a ponytail!'

'Particularly when she grows up to look the way *you* do. What about it, Julia? When may I see you?'

'I'm rather tied up at the moment.'

'A boyfriend? I know you aren't married or Rob would have told me.'

'No, no boyfriend,' she said, 'but I—I've just taken on a job that——' She stopped, knowing she dare not explain, and uncertain what to say. In the end she agreed to meet him at Le Suquet for dinner. It was one of the best fish restaurants in town, and noisy and crowded enough to preclude intimate conversation. After all, how well did she know Chris? He hadn't bothered with her as a teenager, but with these glossy pictures of her as a model firmly fixed in his mind he might now be entertaining far different ideas.

It was an amusing thought, particularly when she remembered how she had once vowed to show him what he had missed! Well, here was her chance. Except it didn't seem important any more. But what the hell! It would be fun seeing him again.

Slipping into a hyacinth-flowered silk dress that deepened the blue in her eyes, she wound her blue-black hair into a coil on the nape of her neck, recollecting how Chris had liked to tug her lanky ponytail. Donning matching blue pumps, she surveyed herself in the mirror. A touch of pink to her cheeks and mouth completed the picture, and, even if she said so herself, she looked a dream. Pity she couldn't look it for someone else. But who? And where to find such a man?

Chris was waiting for her outside the restaurant, tall, blond and handsome as she remembered. Yet not quite as she remembered, for there was no charisma, no force of personality, just a good-looking, fair-haired man. But, if she was disappointed, Chris's look of astonished delight showed *he* wasn't.

'You're beautiful,' he murmured, 'much more beautiful than your photographs.'

'It's lovely to see you.' She brushed his compliment aside and tried not to draw away as he took her arm in a proprietorial gesture and led her into the restaurant.

Even here, where many pretty women congregated, Julia still drew all eyes. But she was used to it and able to ignore it as she draped her wrap over the back of her chair and concentrated on her companion.

'Hey,' she said, 'stop staring at me like that.'

'I can't help it. You're so different. The ugly duckling's become a swan.'

'I was never an ugly duckling,' she reminded him. 'Just the usual scrawny teenager.'

'Sorry!' he grinned. 'But do you think *I've* changed as much as you?'

'Hardly at all.'

'Do you remember the crush you used to have on me?'

'Teenagers don't have much sense,' she laughed, and was amused to see him look put out. 'Tell me about yourself,' she said quickly, knowing that most men—

most people, come to think of it—enjoyed talking about themselves.

She didn't have to ask him twice, for he launched into a blow-by-blow account of what had happened to him since they had last met: his marriage and a job in Sydney which hadn't lasted due to his wanderlust. But he always managed to find something that suited him better, though not better enough to anchor him, and after his sixth move in five years, his wife had tired of the travelling and left him, after which he had drifted some more before returning to London and another excellent job.

'This one I'm really going to stick at,' Chris said. 'Bairstow and Marsh are a top advertising agency, as you know, and with Bob Marsh himself rooting for me, the only way I can go is up.'

'Providing you don't get another attack of wanderlust.'

'A girl like you could turn itchy feet into sticky feet,' he said, leaning across the table. 'You will let me see you again, won't you, Julia?'

She stared into his eyes, waiting to feel that special lift of excitement that always seemed to elude her. As it eluded her this time. 'If I'm free,' she parried. 'I'm starting a rather difficult job and I'm not sure how busy I'll be.'

'I won't take no for an answer.' Chris raised his wineglass to her and Julia raised hers in response. As she did, from the corner of her eye she saw a man on the far side of the room lift *his* glass to her too, and her heart did a flip-flóp as she recognised Rees Denton. What a coincidence! Yet from tomorrow it wouldn't be, for from then on she would have to find out where he was going *every* night and make sure she was to hand. How much simpler her task would be if *she* were his date. No, not 'if', 'when'. For only when she was close to him could she properly protect him.

Under cover of her conversation with Chris, who was happy to go on talking about himself, she surreptitiously watched Rees Denton and the girl with him. A pretty girl who kept patting her curly, blonde hair and simpering up at him. What, for heaven's sake, could an intelligent man like Rees Denton have in common with an idiot like that? Unless it pleased him to know he didn't have to put himself out to please *her*. Well, if *that* was all he wanted... But how was *she* supposed to act stupid when she wasn't?

'You're not listening,' she heard Chris say.

'I'm sorry.' Quickly Julia focused on him as he started asking her what she had been doing in the years since they had met.

'The usual sort of thing,' she said vaguely. 'Some work for a couturier house in Paris and Rome, and then mainly photographic modelling.'

'And at the moment?' Chris asked. 'You said you were doing something difficult.'

She hesitated, then decided to be honest, hardly amazed by his look of incredulity as he heard her out.

'A bodyguard? You? I can't believe it,' he exclaimed.

'Because I'm a woman?'

'Partly. But more because you're—well, you're just not the type. You don't look it, for one thing.'

'All the better to fool people, as the wolf said to Red Riding Hood!'

He chuckled. 'Well, you could certainly have fooled me. Who are you protecting now?'

'You know very well I can't tell you.'

He looked disconcerted, and Julia hurriedly switched the conversation back to himself, which soon restored his humour. It didn't do much for her own, however, for he was not the most scintillating conversationalist and she was soon bored out of her skull. None the less she feigned interest, staring into his eyes and careful not to look Rees Denton's way again. Though, when she finally left the restaurant, a quick glance across the room showed his table occupied by another couple. No prize for guessing what Rees Denton was doing at this moment, nor with whom!

'When can I see you again?' Chris asked as their taxi drew to a stop outside her apartment house and he helped her out.

'Give me a call,' Julia parried.

'I will,' he warned. 'I won't let you escape me again.'

Vowing to keep her answerphone switched on, she lightly kissed him on the cheek, marvelling that she'd ever broken her heart over this blond, handsome giant who now left her completely cold.

That night she dreamt of Rees Denton, a jumble of images that fast receded as she stretched and yawned and opened her eyes to the morning. Throwing off her duvet, she went to the window to let in the daylight and some sanity. She had some tough weeks ahead of her, and must concentrate her energies on not only being an efficient personal assistant, but also the sort of dumb *femme fatale* that Rees Denton found appealing. Yet how to combine an efficient PA with the kind of girl who jumped on a chair if she saw a mouse?

The secret was not to be obvious. She didn't have to look or act the clinging vine for Rees to sit up and take notice of her. Just a hint of helplessness would do. After all, what made a man feel important was to make sure he didn't feel threatened. That was it. She would pander to his every whim and make it clear she considered him the most intelligent, superior being she had ever met. That would soon have him eating out of her hand!

She twisted her hair into the smooth bun she had worn yesterday, then, deciding it suited the PA image but wasn't quite what she wanted, she wound it into a braid and pinned it on top of her head, carefully pulling out a few tendrils to soften the effect. Pleased with the result, for it gave her a Regency air, she padded into the bathroom to dress.

CHAPTER THREE

THE CHANCE to try out her new persona came sooner than Julia anticipated, for on her way up to Rees Denton's office suite the elevator stopped on the third floor to let him in.

'Good morning,' he smiled, the whiteness of his teeth accentuated by his tanned skin.

'Good morning,' she said, moving to the door, poised to step out when the elevator stopped again. But when it did, the doors didn't open, and a glance at the indicator panel showed it had come to a standstill between two floors. She pressed the button, but nothing happened.

'Let me,' Rees Denton said, and tried again without success. 'Damn! It's never done this before.'

Julia glanced up at the roof. The elevator had a false ceiling and she was certain it would undo easily to give access to an emergency exit. From there, it should be possible to reach the exit doors of the next floor. Quick as the idea came to her, so she discounted it, knowing that fate had presented her with a golden opportunity of showing this man how helpless she could be. Without further ado, she gave a pathetic little squeak and flung her arms around his neck.

'I'm frightened,' she cried. 'What if it falls? What's going to happen to us?'

'Nothing that pressing Emergency won't remedy,' he said gently, and, disengaging her arms, did so. Julia was glad she hadn't remembered the Emergency button herself or she would have found it hard to make her frightened act look genuine.

'I'm s-sorry to be so silly,' she whispered. 'But I suffer from claustrophobia.'

'That can be frightening.' His voice held sympathy. 'Why didn't you use the stairs?'

'Up all those flights? Anyway, I can't bear heights either.'

'Not even when you're *inside* a building?'

She gave a fearful shiver. 'Sounds silly, I know, but I keep remembering I'm leaving the ground far below me and—and my feet turn to lead.'

'You should stick to a job on the ground floor, then.'

Was he laughing at her? she wondered, and, studying him through her lashes, saw his face held no expression whatever. But what a handsome face it was! His eyes were dark and bright, his skin clear and glowing with health, giving no indication that he might have had a pretty active night. Her imagination began working overtime and she was glad when the elevator gave a jerk and then glided up to the top floor.

'Mrs Williamson must be wondering what's happened to me,' Julia said as they walked together down the corridor. 'I wouldn't like her to think I'm late on my first morning.'

'I'll see she doesn't,' he replied, and paused as they reached the door of his office suite.

She waited for him to open it, but he blocked the way to prevent her moving past him. 'Are you doing anything tonight, Miss Winterton?'

'Why? Do you want to work late?'

'I'm not anticipating it. But I'd like to take you out to dinner.'

'To dinner?' Julia had difficulty hiding her triumph. Her little-girl act had paid off quicker than she had anticipated; either that, or he was a pushover for a pretty face.

'Do you already have a date?' he asked, noticing her hesitation.

'No, but——'

'Then what's the problem?'

'I've never dated my boss before.'

'There's always a first time.'

Still she hesitated. He obviously wasn't used to women saying 'no' to him, and she would have enjoyed giving him his come-uppance. But she was here for one reason only—to protect this Lothario—and her preferences had to take second place to her duty.

'I'd like to go out with you, Mr Denton, but I'm not dressed for it.'

'You look fine to me.'

'You think so?' she asked coyly.

'I wouldn't say it if I didn't mean it.'

'Do you always say what you mean?'

'Not always,' he said silkily.

'Then how will I know whether to believe you?'

For an instant he looked nonplussed. 'I'm sure you'll manage,' he answered. 'Most women have a highly developed sense of self-preservation which enables them to know when they're being lied to.'

'Lots of wives don't,' she countered, her expression bland. 'One is always reading terrible stories of husbands playing fast and loose and their wives being the last to know.'

'Yes—well—I wasn't talking about wives,' he said. 'Just girlfriends.'

Julia made herself give a girlish giggle, thinking this was the easiest way to change the conversation, and wondered how many times she would have to use it as a ploy.

Rees Denton stepped back to let her precede him into the office, then walked through it into his own, explaining to Mrs Williamson over his shoulder why they had both been delayed.

For the rest of the day the older woman showed Julia what she would have to do in the office, and, though assured that the job wasn't arduous, by six o'clock Julia was in no mood to agree. Apart from taking innumerable telephone calls, she was expected to liaise with the laboratory, the design department and the factory. Mr Denton, she learned, was a high-powered man in a high-powered position. He had a workforce of a thousand men and countless numbers of important clients who all wanted him to solve their particular engineering problems. No wonder Sir Andrew considered his safety to be of prime importance.

'Why are you frowning?' Mrs Williamson asked when the telephones had finally ceased ringing and they were both relaxing in an office that had miraculously gone quiet.

'I'm wondering how to handle the security side of my job. If I often have to take confidential documents from one office to another, Mr Denton will be left unguarded.'

'You're right,' Mrs Williamson ran a hand through her sleek grey hair. 'I'll arrange for you to have an assistant that you can call on.' She scribbled some names on a pad and passed it across to Julia. 'Either of these girls will be happy to help you.' Mrs Williamson stood up and glanced around the room. 'I wonder how long I'll have to stay away from here?'

'Hard to tell,' Julia shrugged. 'But whoever is making these threats against Mr Denton will have to make a move sooner or later, and he knows that the longer he leaves it, the more chance there is of the police laying a trap for him. Anyway, I thought you were going to Canada to see your mother?'

'That was a ruse Sir Andrew dreamt up. My mother's gone on a cruise with her second husband, and wouldn't appreciate a middle-aged daughter playing second fiddle!' Mrs Williamson went to the door leading to Rees Denton's office. 'I'll go in and say goodbye.'

When she emerged she was pink-eyed and carrying a black crocodile cosmetic case. 'What do you think of this?'

Julia's eyes widened as she saw its suede interior was filled with a complete line of Estée Lauder products. What a stupid gift to give a woman who didn't appear to use anything other than lipstick and powder. But, bearing in mind the elaborately made-up creature she had seen with him last night, he probably assumed every woman longed to cover her face with goo.

'It's a wonderful present,' she said diplomatically.

'I can't wait to try everything,' the older woman confessed. 'It's always been a secret dream of mine to have the complete Lauder range, but it seemed too extravagant to treat myself to it.'

Julia silently apologised to the man. Seemed he knew his personal assistant better than she did!

'Are you leaving with me?' Mrs Williamson asked as she reached for her coat and saw Julia still at her desk.

'No. I'm staying until Mr Denton goes.'

'Of course. How silly of me.' She looked over her shoulder, then whispered, 'How will you disguise yourself when you follow him?'

'I won't even try,' Julia grinned. 'I'm not a private eye! But keeping tabs on him *isn't* going to be easy. That's our big problem at the moment, though I've managed to solve it for tonight.'

'How?'

'He's asked me to have dinner with him.'

'I see.'

The dryness of the tone made Julia defensive. 'It's the best way we could think of to keep tabs on him. In the normal course of events, I never date clients.'

Mrs Williamson looked apologetic, as if knowing Julia had guessed what had been going through her mind. 'Such a pity Mr Denton's complicating things with his silly attitude. So much easier if you could tell him who you really are and do your job properly.'

'I've every intention of doing my job properly,' Julia asserted—and of making sure Rees Denton doesn't behave *im*properly, she added to herself, though when he entered her office an hour and a half later, as immaculate as though he had just showered and changed, she wished for the first time that she had met him socially and could be herself. The thought did not please her, for, though she wouldn't be happy working for a client she disliked, it could complicate matters if she liked one too much. Reminding herself that in her real persona, Rees Denton wouldn't fancy her—how could he, when he liked simpering 'yes'-women, more famous for their beauty than their brains?—she also saw it as a warning not to let her emotions run away with her. This was an assignment pure and simple, and when it was over their paths would no longer cross.

'Sorry to keep you waiting,' he said, not looking in the least sorry, 'but I got caught up with a problem and didn't realise how late it was.'

'It's only seven-thirty,' Julia said, though in the normal course of events she would never have waited an hour and a half for *any* date, no matter how gorgeous. 'Where are we going?' she asked as they descended to the basement parking and his low-slung black Ferrari.

'I've booked a table at Tante Claire.'

Julia was impressed but did not show it, for Tante Claire was a three-star restaurant and one had to book weeks in advance. However, remembering the role she was playing, she gave a simpering smile. 'You must be very influential to get a table there at such short notice.'

'I dine there so often, they always give me preference.'

'How lovely to be so well-known.'

He gave her a sharp look, but she kept hers wide-eyed and innocent, and he relaxed. 'If you'd rather go somewhere else . . .' he murmured.

'Oh, no! I'd be crazy not to want to go *there*,' she cooed. 'I've heard it's beautiful.'

'So are you,' he smiled, holding the car door open for her to slide into the passenger seat.

She didn't answer, nor did he talk again as they drove to the restaurant. As far back as her teens, when she had driven with one or other of her brothers, she had been aware how differently people controlled a car, and how much of their character they disclosed when they did. Like Rees Denton, for example, who handled his with confidence and ease, never exceeding the speed limit, which must be difficult in a car that touched a hundred and twenty before you could count to five, never overtaking unless the road was absolutely clear, yet giving one the feeling that if need be he could drive this superb piece of mechanism to its utmost limit and still look as nonchalant about it as if he were doing a steady thirty.

When they entered the restaurant, Julia received the usual appreciative male glances. But there was a difference, for she received intent female glances too, as her companion was assessed and sighed over. It wasn't surprising though, for it was not only his looks that attracted attention, but his air of command. She wondered if he had always had it, or whether it came with success, and debated whether she dared ask him about himself or whether it was too much out of character in the part she was playing. She thought of some of the model girls she had known, in particular the silly ones who had been nothing more than clothes-horses, and knew they would never have been sufficiently interested in a man to find out what he thought and how he felt—other than how he thought and felt about them!

They were shown to a corner table, and Rees Denton immediately asked her what she would like to drink.

'*You* decide,' she simpered, for though it was a rule that a Guardian Security officer did not drink on the job, she intended putting him through the hoop.

'Don't you have any preference?' he asked.

'Not really.'

'Well, let me see—gin and tonic?'

'I hate gin and tonic.'

'Vodka?'

'Ugh!'

'A whisky, then.'

'I never drink whisky.'

'How about some wine?'

It was just what she fancied, but she resisted the temptation. 'I don't really like alcohol,' she lied, and had the pleasure of seeing a spasm of irritation cross his face. Equally quickly she batted her long lashes at him, and his eyes widened as if they had actually struck him!

'A fruit juice, then?' he asked gently.

'Lovely,' she breathed.

She behaved with equal stupidity over the menu, but not by a flicker did Rees Denton show irritation at having to explain every item to her. Even when he had to listen to her inane conversation all evening he kept his patience, and she decided he was too good to be true. Except he liked his women dumb, didn't he? She stifled a smile. Who would have guessed that security work included acting stupid? It needed guts, fitness and fire, but *stupidity*?

'Where do you live?' he asked as they drained the last of their coffee.

'Sloane House,' she said without thinking, and only when she saw one dark eyebrow rise in astonishment did she realise it was far too expensive an address for any personal assistant, however well paid, to afford. Her brain raced. 'I—er—I'm staying there rent-free. The owner's gone abroad and I'm house-sitting for an old lady.' That would at least explain away the lovely antique pieces and the fine Stubbs that hung above her mantelpiece, a present from her parents on her twenty-first birthday.

'Very clever of you,' Rees Denton said. 'I know it's hard finding decent accommodation at an affordable rent.' He signalled for the bill. 'Your place or mine?'

The inference was obvious, and in the normal course of events Julia would have made it plain it was neither place! With swift realisation she acknowledged that this job wasn't going to be a walkover, and that it would require all her finesse to keep this man at bay without antagonising him.

So what to do now? If she invited him into *her* apartment, he would have to return home alone, yet if she went to his he was sufficient of a gentleman to drive her home afterwards. Deciding to cross that bridge when she came to it, she simpered, '*Your* place.'

Only when they were in the car did she realise she didn't know where 'his place' was. What if he lived out of town, miles from a cab rank? Still, if he came on too strongly, she could be even stronger. She mustn't start thinking she was the simpering fool she was pretending to be. She was perfectly capable of taking care of herself.

In fact, she was trained to do so, and could hold her own with a man twice her size and weight.

Twenty minutes later they entered the Dockside apartment block where he lived, only a few streets away from the bronze façade of Engineering 2000, and took the elevator up to his tenth floor penthouse.

Julia stifled a gasp as they entered the domed, marble-floored hall and Rees turned on the concealed lighting. It suffused the entire area in a mellow glow, lighting up a central glass table banked with flowers, as well as the living-room beyond. She had not pictured his home like this, imagining it would be masculine and sombre, rather than so designer-decorated.

There was glass everywhere; from the mirrored walls to the multi-faceted screen that partitioned the living and dining areas, where the only concessions to warmth were the soft leather chairs surrounding a black glass and steel dining-table.

But she was being unfair. For the living-room itself was welcoming and warm, despite the angularity of its shape, with silk-textured fabrics in shades of ivory and peach upholstering the deep settees and armchairs, as well as the walls.

But it was the wall of glass at the far end that drew her, for through it she had a spectacular view of the river, gleaming like a black satin ribbon. She could well imagine the daytime picture, and wondered if she would see it. But she would definitely have to, *day and night*, if she wanted to keep Rees alive.

'Stunning, isn't it?' he said behind her, taking the wrap from around her and kissing the side of her neck.

'Stunning,' she echoed.

'It's even better by day.' He pointed to the telescope on a tripod in the corner. 'I only wish I had more time to use it. But what will you have to drink?'

'Orange juice.' She moved away from him and perched on the edge of an armchair.

'Again?'

'I was brought up on orange juice,' she said innocently.

'But you're a big girl now. You should try living dangerously.'

'Why? I'm happy as I am.'

'A little danger adds spice to the gingerbread.'

'I hate gingerbread.'

He gave a mock sigh. 'I give up on you, Julia.'

'I'm glad to hear that, Mr Denton.'

'Rees,' he corrected. 'Why do you find it so hard to say?'

'I don't. But you're my employer and it doesn't seem——'

'Right? How old-fashioned of you! These days people are on first-name terms the moment they meet. But to get back to what you said just before. Why were you glad when I said I give up on you?'

Julia hesitated. She wanted to say 'because you're a devilishly handsome man and I think you'd be a devil to love, and give any girl crazy enough to fall for you a lot of heartache'. But she knew she couldn't be honest, for she had to inveigle herself into his life and spend as much time with him as possible. Which would be all too easy to do, she knew, noting the gleam in his eye. But if she did, where would professionalism end and her own emotions take over? It was a question she dare not answer, for as of now her professionalism was at stake, and that meant having to disregard her personal feelings.

'Do you really want me to give up on you?' he repeated.

'Perhaps you shouldn't be such a fast worker,' she murmured. 'You're inclined to—to rush a girl off her feet.'

'Once I know what I want, I don't see the point in beating around the bush.'

'And I'm the particular bush you want to pick?'

'Yes,' he chuckled. 'A very decorative one, too.'

'But most bushes are perennial and you only want annuals. Or perhaps I should say monthlies.'

'Very clever, Julia. You're not so dumb, after all!'

'My mother's a keen gardener,' Julia said hastily, knowing she had to watch her tongue. 'Anyway, a girl doesn't have to be all that clever to see through you, Mr Denton.'

'Rees,' he reminded, handing her an orange juice.

Accepting it, she glanced round the room. 'Did you design all this yourself?'

'No. A friend of mine did.'

'Someone you know well?'

'That's an odd question.' He seemed amused by it.

'Only because I don't think it suits you.'

'Most people think it matches my personality exactly.'

'Well, I don't. It's too artificial, and you're very much a cards on the table man, with a firm set of principles.'

'Indeed? I've been told I can be devious, subtle and ruthless.'

'Only when you have to be. But by nature you prefer being honest.'

'That's a charming compliment, Julia. I shall treasure it.'

She pretended unawareness of the humour in his tone, but she had decided—on the spur of the moment—to let him think she saw him as an honourable man who would appreciate her innocence, in the hope that this would encourage him to actually do so!

'You know, there's something in what you say,' he murmured. 'I'm not quite the big bad wolf this décor implies. So you needn't perch on the edge of that chair like a nervous sparrow. After all, *you're* not quite what you seem, either?'

Her heart leapt into her throat. Oh, lord! He had guessed what she was. But how? 'I—I'm not?' she queried.

'Definitely not. When Mrs Williamson recommended you, she informed me you were a highly capable PA, and that being the case, you can't be the innocent you pretend.'

'By innocent, I suppose you mean virginal?'

Rees was momentarily nonplussed. 'Well, yes.'

'That's stupid reasoning, if you don't mind my saying so. Why can't a successful career girl also remain a virgin?'

'I suppose she could if she were fat and ugly. But you're a beautiful, sexy girl, and I don't believe I'm the first man who has lusted after you.'

This was pretty straight talking, and Julia longed to tell him exactly what he could do with his lust! But she had to tread carefully.

'I'd never go to bed with a man unless we were in love with each other. I'm not interested in casual sex.'

'Nor am I.' Rees came to stand in front of her. 'Casual sex is too dangerous. Anyway, one-night stands are boring when you're over thirty.'

It was a good line, but she didn't believe him. How could she, when she had done her best to be inane and trivial? 'You'd find *me* very boring,' she pouted.

'I find you an enigma,' he corrected. 'The glowing reference from Mrs Williamson doesn't tally with your—er—your——'

'Intelligence?' This time she finished *his* sentence. 'It's easy for me to be a good assistant, because I regard my boss as my child and do everything I can to mother him.'

'Mother him?' Rees was staggered.

'All the time. Mother him, protect him, make sure he has everything he wants when he wants it.'

'Well, you know what *I* want!' He reached for her, and with an effort she made herself stay where she was and not hit out at him. 'Julia, darling, why waste time talking when we can be——'

'We can't,' she cut in. 'It's the wrong time of the month.'

It was an effort not to laugh at the expression on his face, and she made a mental note to recount it to Murray. For the first time since accepting this assignment, she saw it might have its funny moments.

'That's a very good excuse,' he said, stepping away from her. 'But only a temporary one. Now, drink up and I'll take you home.'

'There's no need. I'll get a cab.'

'I'll ring for one,' he said promptly.

She had expected him to argue and, when he didn't, was irrationally disappointed, for it showed he wanted her for one thing only. When she hadn't given it to him, he couldn't wait to be rid of her. Yet, had he taken her home, she would have had to follow him back in her own car to make sure he wasn't attacked, so it was all to the good that he was such a swine!

He put down the telephone and picked up her wrap.

'You're not angry with me?' she asked softly as he draped it round her.

'Of course not.'

'Then you'll ask me out again?'

'Of course,' he said politely.

That means he won't, she thought, and tantalisingly licked her lower lip with the tip of her tongue. 'I'm sorry I had to say no to you.' She felt rather than saw his interest reawaken, and hid her triumph.

'Don't give it a thought,' he said huskily. 'There'll be other occasions.'

Thankfully the buzz of the intercom signalled the arrival of her cab, and she walked quickly through the hall to the elevator.

'Don't bother coming downstairs with me,' she said as he went to follow her into it. The assassin could be lurking outside, and he would be far safer if he stayed in his high-tech ivory tower.

'Don't be silly,' he replied. 'Of course I'll see you down.'

She thought wildly. 'No, you mustn't. I don't want the cab driver to know I'm leaving a man's apartment.'

Rees gaped at her. 'In this day and age?'

'I'm sorry, but that's the way I feel.'

'You could always tell him you were taking dictation!'

'I don't think he'd believe me,' Julia said primly, and pressed the button.

Only as the door closed did she allow herself a huge grin. It was fun acting dumb, and might become even funnier, though she was determined that the laugh—when it finally came—would be on Rees Denton.

Mind, it wasn't going to be easy holding him off, and if the worst came to the worst she would come clean and tell him the truth. But for as long as possible she would maintain her charade, and hope that, before it grew too difficult to play, the person threatening his life would be safely behind bars.

CHAPTER FOUR

NEXT morning in the office Rees reverted to his role of managing director, neither by word nor gesture indicating he had taken her to dinner the previous night and asked to go to bed with her.

She knew he would pose the question again, but for the moment she put it from her mind and concentrated on keeping alert, hoping she might notice someone or something suspicious. The police believed, as did the directors of this company, that a bereaved next-of-kin was behind the death threats made to Rees, but Julia was still watchful of all the personnel around her, deciding it was better to be safe than sorry.

Guarding Rees during the day would present little problem, for as his assistant she could accompany him most places. Not that she would need to when he was in the building, for he was always with other engineers and technicians or his fellow directors. And, since his lunches were generally working ones, her real problems would only start when his working day was over.

Apart from a meeting with Sir Andrew that morning, where Rees had introduced her to him, and Sir Andrew had greeted her as though she were a complete stranger, he had remained at his drawing-board in his office. So without worry, she put her head around his door at lunch time to say she was off to the canteen and would be back within the hour.

'Don't rush,' he replied. 'I'm lunching with one of the engineers and don't expect to be back before three-thirty.'

'Does that mean you'll be working late tonight?'

'I doubt it.'

Julia went off to the canteen, then decided to stretch her legs and go for a walk instead. She could always munch an apple or two on the way. Singing softly under her breath, for it was a lovely day and this was, after all, her first job of any importance, she sauntered down the steps of the building and had almost reached the last one when she espied Rees climbing into a sleek red convertible, an equally sleek blonde at the wheel. The same blonde she had seen dining with him at Le Suquet the night before last.

Lunching with one his engineers, was he? The lying toad! No wonder he had said he wouldn't be back till half-past three. There was no prize for guessing how he would be occupied!

She was on the verge of telling herself it was none of her business what he did with his life, when she recollected that it was. Dammit, she was here to protect him, and that meant watching him the whole time. But how could she? She was no Peeping Tom!

She was still mulling over the problem when she re-entered the office, though it was after four before Rees came in, his step jaunty.

'Had a good lunch?' she asked icily.

'Very.' He paused by his door. 'Why the glacial tone?'

'I beg your pardon?'

'No need to do that,' he said jovially. 'Just tell me why you've gone frigid on me.'

Knowing she dared not, she contented herself with a shrug.

'Dog-in-the-mangerish, are we?' he went on. 'Funny, I'd never have taken you for the jealous type.'

Even as she looked up indignantly, he had closed the door behind him, and Julia was sorely tempted to walk out there and then, except she wasn't one to leave a sinking ship. Hell, Rees was the rat, not her! But, regardless of this, she didn't want him shot down in cold blood.

Promptly at six he walked into her office. 'Still angry, Julia?'

'I never was,' she replied, looking up coolly from her word processor.

'In that case, will you have dinner with me again tonight?'

She almost obliterated a whole paragraph. 'Dinner with you?'

'Yes, and forget about Dawn.' He perched on her desk.

'Dawn?' Julia made her voice rise on the question, though she knew exactly who he meant, for the name suited her to a T.

'The girl you saw me with today.'

'I didn't——'

'You did,' he corrected. 'I saw you out the corner of my eye.'

'How odd. I thought they were both fixed on your ladyfriend! She's certainly pretty enough,' Julia made herself add.

'And pretty dumb.'

'You think the same of me,' Julia said sadly.

'Not quite. *You* make me laugh.'

Oh, but he was quick off the mark! Julia couldn't help admiring him, even though she knew his expertise came from a great deal of practice.

'Do you like notching up new conquests on your belt?' she asked blandly.

'I've never done it on a belt, sweet Julia. On a bed, on a couch, on a rug, on a——'

'No more!' she cried, clapping her hands to her ears. But his answer showed her all too clearly that if she didn't infiltrate herself into his life she'd be spending a whole lot of hers pacing the pavements outside elegant houses or apartments, watching curtained windows! Yet there had to be a way of getting close to him without being too close for comfort, though as of now she couldn't think of one.

'So what's it to be?' he asked impatiently. 'May I see you tonight or not?'

'If not, will it be with someone else?'

'Definitely. I'm in the mood for dancing. So it's you or Dawn or anyone else who's free.'

'Not very choosy, are you?'

'I happen to be very choosy,' he replied loftily. 'All the women in my little black book are highly desirable.'

'And willing,' Julia added.

'Of course. But I make it a policy to take no for an answer.'

'Would you put that in writing?'

'Certainly not!' He leaned across the desk, one lean finger coming up to tilt her chin. 'Don't take life so seriously, sweetie. It's all a game, and you and I could play very nicely together.'

'I'd rather dance,' she said pertly.

'Then go home and change and I'll pick you up at eight-thirty.'

That meant he would be driving home alone, parking his car below the block where he lived—and a damned big, eerie car park it was, too—then going up in the elevator which might stop at one of the floors to let in his assailant. Oh, no! it didn't bear thinking of. She had to find a way of being with him far more than she was.

'Why don't I go back home with you and wait while *you* change?' she suggested. 'Then you can drive me home and wait while *I* change. It will save me going on the train.'

He looked surprised by the suggestion. 'I thought I'd shower and have a rest.'

'You still can. I don't mind watching television.'

He narrowed his eyes at her. 'You're a funny girl, Julia.'

'No, I'm not. I just suffer from claustrophobia, and I'd rather sit in your car than in the tube.'

'Ah,' he said ruefully. 'For a minute I thought you were making a pass at me!'

'I'd never do that. I'm a good girl, Rees.'

His mouth twitched, but his voice was serious as he answered, 'I'm glad to hear it. In fact, I think you'd be very good.'

She lowered her eyes to hide the amusement in them, and gave him full marks for never giving up.

Back in his apartment he was as good as his word, giving her a large glass of fresh orange juice and then leaving her to watch television while he went off to shower and rest.

'I'll only sleep for an hour,' he assured her, 'then I'll take you home to change.'

'You can sleep for longer,' Julia said quickly, thinking how marvellous it would be if he slept away the whole evening, and saved her from simpering and giggling away the next four hours. But it was not to be, for, saying he would be fit as a fiddle after a short nap, he took himself off.

Alone, Julia relaxed, switching off the television and quietly sipping her fruit juice before wandering around the apartment. She wasn't being idly curious, she told herself. It was simply sensible to know the lie of the land:

to see where entry could be made, and which part of the apartment was more vulnerable than another.

In the event, the security was excellent, with alarms fitted to all windows and doors, which could be activated when Rees was out or asleep, and twenty-four-hour alarms on the back and front doors. But no security, however strong, could prevent a determined person from gaining entry, and for this reason she couldn't help being uneasy as to Rees' safety when he was here in the evenings and at weekends. She would ask Murray if he had any suggestions. In fact, she might as well talk to him now. But first she had better make sure Rees was asleep.

Tiptoeing down the marble corridor to his bedroom, she put her ear to the door. Then, to be safe rather than sorry, she gingerly turned the handle, praying the door wouldn't squeak. But it glided smoothly open—naturally it would in such a luxury apartment—and she had her first glimpse of Rees in bed.

It was seven foot wide, its bronze, fan-shaped headboard matching the bronze and smoky-grey glass bedside-tables. The carpet was darker grey, thick and luxurious, and was complimented by pearlised blue-grey walls, lacquered at least ten times, Julia guessed, to give them such wonderful iridescence. Heavy satin curtains were so identical in colour to the walls that it was only the thickness of the material that brought them to the eye.

They were undrawn, and she saw the darkening sky and the gleaming lights of the lamps on the riverbanks. But, beautiful though the room was, it was Rees who held her attention, his body half covered by a light duvet, patterned in grey and bronze silk. Unable to stop herself, she tiptoed closer, then stopped suddenly, colour flaming her cheeks as she realised he was sleeping in the raw. Still, the duvet covered the essential parts of him, and anyway she'd seen her four brothers in the nude often enough. But Rees wasn't her brother. Also, he had his own brand of good looks. Not the outdoor type, like Jack and Mark and Rob, nor tall and rangy like Dean. No, Rees' physique was less obvious, though equally strong and masculine, with wide shoulders and smooth chest tapering to a narrow waist. His thighs and loins were covered, thank goodness, but he'd flung out one leg restlessly, and she glimpsed the sinewy muscles of his calf and a beautifully formed foot.

In repose he looked younger, less hard-bitten, and there was an unexpected softness to his mouth. Normally set in sardonic lines, it showed gentle curves in sleep; nor had she noticed how long his lashes were and how translucent his lids. They were shadowed blue, and she knew that he drove himself too hard, working and playing with equal fury.

She wished she knew more about his background, then instantly wished she didn't. Murray was always warning them of the dangers of becoming emotionally involved with their clients. 'Liking them too much won't help you take better care of them. On the contrary, it could be the reverse. You must at all times remain calculating and aloof. Calculating in the sense of weighing up what the assailant might do and how you can best circumvent it.'

Remembering this, she walked out of the bedroom and softly closed the door, then returned to the living-room to dial Murray.

To her dismay she learned he had gone abroad to meet a client, which meant that her problem was still hers to solve, and she was cogitating on it when the soft glow of the lights around her brightened, and she swung round to see Rees coming towards her.

As always, she was struck by his looks. Beautiful almost, except that was too feminine a word for a man of such virile masculinity. He looked as rested as though he had slept the night through rather than only an hour, and as he poured himself a whisky—small amount of alcohol and large amount of soda water, she noted—she admired the fluid movements of his body, enhanced by his superlatively cut dark blue suit. His white shirt made his tanned skin appear darker, and as his eyes narrowed as they rested on her she suddenly imagined him in satin doublet and hose, striding the deck of a pirate ship.

Irritated by her fanciful thoughts, she shook her head, and he burst out laughing.

'What's funny?' she asked.

'You,' Rees said. 'I haven't posed any questions yet, but you're already saying "no"!'

She laughed too and rose, and he led the way out.

The rush-hour traffic had long since gone, and in less than half an hour Julia was unlocking her own front door and ushering Rees into her home. No, not mine, she reminded herself. I'm house-sitting and I'd better not forget it.

'Nice place,' Rees commented, crossing the small, square hall and following her into the sitting-room. His eyes took in the several beautiful pieces of antique furniture, the glass shelves either side of the fireplace that held her budding collection of art deco vases and bowls, and the Stubbs above the mantelpiece. It was this that commanded his attention, and he strode over and stared at it.

'Marvellous,' he murmured. 'Your old lady must be well off.'

For an instant Julia thought he was referring to her mother, then realised he meant the mythical old dear she was supposed to be house-sitting for. Oh, lord, she hoped she hadn't left any tell-tale evidence of her own real self lying around! She was reading a book on Modern Philosophers at the moment and, if Rees glimpsed it, it might arouse his curiosity. Her eyes darted around the room and she saw the book in question lying on the settee.

'I must rest for a minute,' she exclaimed, and, flopping down on the corner of the couch, managed to slip the book under the cushions.

'If you're too tired to go dancing, we could stay here,' Rees said, promptly sitting beside her.

Instantly she jumped up. 'I'm fine now.'

His startled expression nearly made her laugh, and she headed for the door. 'Now it's your turn to watch telly,' she called over her shoulder. 'I'll be as quick as I can.'

'There's no hurry,' he replied, and she glanced across at him uncertainly. But he meant it, for he was leaning back, relaxed and at ease, and she suddenly realised this was one of his strengths, an ability to switch off completely and slow himself down.

Pity she couldn't do the same, she thought, as she raced through a shower and into fresh underthings. Only when it came to a dress did she hesitate. She had so many lovely, sophisticated clothes to choose from, yet didn't think this would suit her simpleton image. But what the hell! Even dumb-bells could dress in a sophisticated manner, and she reached for a stark, black crêpe. A wisp of nothing in her hand, on her body it was quite something, caressing every curve and indent of her slender but luscious body, whispering deliciously against her long legs as she slipped on high-heeled black sandals and picked up her purse.

If she needed confirmation that she looked sensational, Rees' look of stunned appreciation more than gave it as he rose slowly to his feet and moved towards her.

'You're quite the most beautiful girl I've seen,' he said huskily.

'Clothes maketh the woman,' she quipped.

'Not in your case. I bet you'd look even better without any!'

She made herself giggle. 'Naughty, naughty. You mustn't say things like that to me.'

'I could say a lot of other things if you'd let me.'

'Well, I won't. And if you don't behave yourself, I won't go out with you.'

'I promise to be as good as you want me to be.'

'Very good,' she said, and, twining her hand through his arm, urged him out.

Driving across the West End to Marco's, the latest place to dine and dance, Julia wondered how she could bear to go on playing the dumb brunette, fearing that if she was too boring she might turn him off. Yet she couldn't suddenly become clever. Maybe she would let herself be less silly. After all, bearing in mind Mrs Williamson had recommended her, Rees shouldn't be surprised if she occasionally showed a flash of sense.

'Why the sigh?' He broke into her thoughts.

'I was thinking of you,' Julia said honestly, 'and wishing I could be more relaxed with you.'

'You mean you aren't?' He seemed genuinely surprised, and taking heart from it she nodded.

'From your reputation, I think you like women who do as they're told and don't give you an argument. And that's not me.'

'Then argue with me,' he chuckled.

'You won't ask me out again if I do.'

'You're maligning me, Julia.' He slowed at a red light. 'You make me sound as if I think of one thing only.'

'Don't you?'

'Definitely not. I appreciate good conversation, and if a woman can hold her own with me, then——'

'I'm so happy you said that,' Julia cut in before he could elaborate. He had given her the opening she wanted and she took it with both hands. 'It's wonderful to meet a man who's willing to talk to me as an equal. I so want us to be friends.'

'So do I,' he said fervently.

'I mean real friendship,' she persisted. 'Not one with sexual undertones.'

The Ferrari spurted forward almost as if in anger, and Julia put a hand to her mouth to hide a smile. '*Will* you be my friend, Rees?'

'Of course. Though you know I'd like more than that.'

'I know. But don't rush me.'

'You have my promise.'

Julia's eyes glittered. The sucker! He had made a statement and she intended nailing him to it.

'I think you must have gone out with some very peculiar men in your time,' he said suddenly. 'You talk as if we're all just waiting to pounce and seduce.'

'The ones I've met *are*,' Julia retorted with genuine feeling.

'I'm not one of them,' Rees asserted, and Julia, glancing at his face, saw he really believed what he was saying. But then, maybe he didn't need to pounce or seduce. He was handsome and eligible enough for the woman to do the pouncing!

For the rest of the evening Rees' behaviour was faultless, though he did hold her a shade too close when they were dancing, and let his fingers linger around her waist as he led her back to their table. But his conversation was strictly impersonal, though occasionally his eyes, glowing like dark coals, said much more.

It was after midnight before he brought her home. And though she said goodnight to him firmly in the car, he was beside her in the elevator as she went up to her apartment.

With her key in the door, she said goodnight to him again, and once again found him beside her in her hallway.

'It's far too late for you to come in for a drink,' she protested.

'I agree. And a drink isn't what I have in mind.' Gently he pushed her into the living-room.

'I'm too tired to talk.'

'Me too,' he said, lowering his mouth to hers as he drew her down with him on to the settee.

Anger flared in her and she held herself aloof from his touch, hoping that if she remained motionless he would get the message. But he was too aroused to receive messages, too intent on his own wants to realise she did not want it at all. So much for his promise!

'You're so beautiful,' he breathed against her lips, as his hand traced a feathery path down her back to her waist, rested there a second, then moved up to cup one breast. 'Beats me why I haven't seen you around before.'

'Maybe because I don't go around.' Julia managed to avert her head. 'Please, Rees, it's late and I want you to go home.'

'Come with me.'

'No.'

'Then let me stay here. I promise I'll only hold you.'

Lord, the times she'd heard that! She pushed against his chest, but he wouldn't budge. 'Rees, go,' she insisted. 'You're breaking your promise.'

'No, I'm not. I'm only holding you and kissing you. A prosaic little kiss between friends.' Tilting her chin, he turned her face to his, and, before she could protest, covered her mouth again. His touch was gentle yet firm, his tongue edging out to savour her lips. Feeling its warmth, she trembled, and the pressure of his mouth grew more insistent, forcing hers apart to give him entry.

She tried to draw back, but as she did he bent with her, and she found herself lying on the cushions with Rees' body covering hers. Through the thin silk of her dress his arousal was all too evident, the throb and heat of it pressing against her thigh. But she experienced none of the anger she normally felt in this sort of situation; instead she was overcome by a sudden longing to draw him closer, to touch her hands to the perfect symmetry of his face, with its broad brow and high cheekbones, to let her fingers knead the muscles of his neck and shoulders, lose themselves in the dark whorls of hair on his chest which she could feel through his fine cambric shirt.

Aware that her resolve was slackening, Rees' kiss deepened, his tongue in her mouth performing the action that the throbbing muscle between his legs so ached to do. As she ached to let him, Julia acknowledged, and was instantly horrified with herself. Rees was a client. She dared not have an affair with him. More important, he was a womaniser, out for what he could get. Dammit! He barely knew her, yet he was falling over himself to get her into bed. Anger dissolved her desire and she longed to throw him out. Even as she tensed to do so, she knew she was duty bound to protect his life, and that she would have to protect her honour in a more subtle way. She racked her brains to figure out how, when she remembered a trick she had learned from Murray to deter unwanted males.

Clasping Rees close in a play of passion, she put her arms around his neck and gently stroked the back of it. At her touch, he groaned deep in his throat, and for an instant she hesitated, reluctant to hurt him, yet accepting she had no choice. Her hand continued its stroking, moving gently backwards and forwards across his neck. Then carefully she pressed.

As if stung by a viper, Rees shot off the settee. 'What the hell was that?'

'What?' she asked innocently. 'Did I do something?'

'*Do* something?' He glared down at her, nursing the back of his neck. 'Stop looking at me with those big eyes of yours! You know damn well what you did.'

'I was only stroking you. Did I scratch you, then? Let me kiss it better.'

'Don't touch me!' he said, though he sounded less angry and more puzzled.

Poor Rees. He didn't know what had hit him! Still, she hadn't pressed as hard as she could have done, so he had been let off lightly!

He kneeled down beside her and she tensed. 'Let me stay with you,' he murmured.

'It's so late.'

'Then we'll go to bed.'

'I can't. I told you it's the wrong time of the month.'

'You said that last night.'

'And I'll have to say it again tomorrow!' Delicately she licked her lips, knowing it was a gesture that never failed to arouse a susceptible male, and Rees, assertive and in control in his business-life, seemed to be a pushover sexually.

She was proved right, for desire flared in the dark depths of his eyes, and though he still looked regretful he accepted her reason for refusing. Gently pulling her to her feet, he kissed her on the forehead, then reached for his jacket, which he had flung on the chair.

'I'll see you down to your car,' Julia said as he reached the front door.

'Don't be silly.'

'But I'd like to.'

He didn't argue, though when she wanted to walk outside the foyer and see him into his Ferrari, he shook his head. 'That dress barely covers you.' He smiled. 'You'll freeze if you go out.'

She nodded as though agreeing with him, but when he opened the car door she was beside him, her body shielding his, did he but know it!

'Get back inside,' he ordered, giving her a gentle push.

She stepped away from the car, and as it roared off into the night she dashed across the road to where she had parked her own, sending up a prayer of thanks for having had the foresight not to garage it.

Because Rees didn't know what car she drove, she was able to follow him closely, donning a rain-hood to partially hide her face in case he glimpsed her through his rear-view mirror. She had watched many car chases on film, and found it far less easy than it looked, for Rees always managed to make the lights before they turned red, forcing her to cross against them. Eventually they reached Dockside, and she watched the Ferrari disappear into the underground parking.

Would he notice her if she followed him inside? Yet no way could he be left unguarded in that vast, cavernous place, and she drove swiftly down the ramp, praying that curiosity wouldn't make him pause when he saw a car close on his heels. But she was in luck, for he parked on the far side, close to one of the elevators, and disappeared into it as she slowly cruised past, head lowered to hide her face.

As the elevator door closed behind him, a shadow moved, and she stopped with a squeal of brakes and dashed out. But there was no one there. She looked around and, still unsatisfied, headed for the exit door, taking the stairs two at a time to the lobby, where she was able to get another elevator that took her swiftly to the penthouse floor.

Stepping into the corridor, she found it empty, and she tiptoed to Rees' door and put her ear to it. All was silent. But that didn't mean someone couldn't be in there with him, brandishing a silencer! Heart hammering, she stood listening, but the silence continued—which could mean nothing or anything! Reluctantly she returned to her car, thankful she had a telephone there and could call him.

'Yes?' he said into the receiver.

'It's me, Julia. I was checking to see you arrived home safely.'

'Sweet of you, but unnecessary. I'm a big boy.'

She made herself giggle, and with a husky 'goodnight' put down the receiver. At least he was safe, but there would be other nights when it mightn't be so easy to keep tabs on him, and she knew it was a problem she had to resolve if she didn't want a dead man on her hands.

CHAPTER FIVE

FIRMLY ensconced in Rees' employ, Julia had to keep reminding herself it wasn't for real. Although she had never worked in an office, the typing course she had taken during a temporary lull in her modelling career was now invaluable, and her natural intelligence helped her cope with Rees' many appointments, as well as keeping at bay all the people he did not want to see. If only it were as easy for her to keep his would-be assassin away from him!

Julia used every possible pretext to stick as close to him as possible, afraid that if she didn't she might find him lying in a pool of blood and she grappling with a maniac!

It was a good thing Murray was not party to her thoughts, for he would have laughed himself silly, or else been furious with her. After all, a bodyguard should be cool and calm, not go around double-checking doors, locks and windows every few hours, nor bite her nails with fear when Rees had lunch in the directors' dining-room, or spent hours in the laboratory on the third floor, or drove to the company's engineering works outside London.

Indeed, when he was there, he was probably safest of all, for the factory was heavily guarded to prevent their designs being copied or stolen, and, as Sir Andrew himself had told Julia on one occasion when Rees was out of earshot, not even a fly could get through their security.

Rees never referred to the threats made against him, but she knew they had all been made via the telephone, and one afternoon, when she had been working for him for nearly two weeks, she casually asked him whether the voice was male or female.

'Who told you about the calls?' he asked tersely, swivelling round from his desk to glare at her.

'Mrs Williamson,' Julia lied.

'Then forget it. I've more to do with my time than waste it talking about some madman.'

'But was it a man's voice or a woman's?' she persisted.

'How do I know? It was a whisper.'

None the wiser, Julia left him. Rees had informed her he was working late this evening, and with her dictaphone cleared of all his letters, thanks to the help of the capable secretary Mrs Williamson had arranged to help her, Julia had little to do except twiddle her thumbs. But not wishing Rees to know, for he assumed she did all his typing, she sat at the word processor aimlessly tapping the keys, and was wondering whether she dared bring a book with her to read, when the telephone rang.

Rees must have been expecting a call, for he picked it up the same time she did, and before she could replace it, she heard a whispering voice. Immediately her hand stilled, and she listened in, her heart racing madly as a low voice—male, she was sure—uttered its spine-chilling threat.

'Your days are numbered, Mr Denton,' it said. 'If you think you can get away from me, forget it. I know your every move.' Click and silence.

Without thinking, Julia rushed into Rees, but, far from finding him white-faced and shaken, he had resumed work, his sleek dark head bent over some technical drawings.

'Rees!' Julia said urgently. 'That man wasn't joking.'

'So?'

'So what are you going to do?'

'Carry on studying these drawings, if you'd be kind enough to let me. If I took notice of every maniac who——'

'But you must!' she cried.

'I *must* have a cup of coffee, with one of those shortbreads Mrs Williamson has tucked away in the tin in the bottom drawer of her desk!'

Exasperated, Julia glared at him, determined to say something to penetrate that thick skull of his! 'You can't ignore that lunatic, Rees!'

'I can and will. Now, stop over-reacting.'

'Only if you stop under-reacting, or are you so intent on preserving your macho image that you're willing to behave like a fool?'

With a deep sigh Rees flung down his pen and swivelled his chair to face her. In dark, hip-fitting trousers and pale blue shirt, sleeves rolled to the elbow to show muscular arms, he emanated an intense aura of strength which was, in an odd way, heightened by his silky, dark hair, dishevelled where he had run his fingers through it.

Julia noted all this in one swift glance, and though she personally wanted a man to have more than just looks, she could not help conceding he was most girls idea of Prince Charming, even though at the moment he was acting more like Prince Irritable!

'OK, Julia,' he said, leaning back in his chair and giving her his version of undivided attention—slightly mocking, as if talking to a child. 'What do you suggest I do?'

'Employ a bodyguard.'

'That's definitely out.'

'Then do you know someone who could be with you the whole time?'

'My little black book is full of numbers,' he chuckled.

'It's no laughing matter,' she said crossly.

'It is, when you start flapping round me like an agitated hen. Anyway, I wouldn't burden my friends with such nonsense.'

'Then let *me* stay with you and watch over you,' she said, grabbing at the chance.

'You?' For a long moment dark eyes held violet ones, hers pleading, his slowly starting to gleam with mischief. 'Well, well,' he drawled, 'now you're really talking. So you're willing to stay with me night and day to protect me, is that it?'

Julia bit her lip. What joy to wipe the look of smug anticipation from his face. But, having got this far...

'Yes,' she stated firmly. 'I'm not as fragile as I appear.'

'Care to put it to the test?'

It was a temptation to say 'yes' and use her hard-won skill as a karate expert to throw him to the ground. But she couldn't allow herself such luxury—at least, not if she wanted to go on working for Guardians—and she contented herself with looking rueful as she murmured, 'I'm not offering my strength, Rees, only my alertness. I know I'm not clever, but I've excellent eyesight and hearing, and I——'

'You also have perfect teeth and a wonderful body,' he cut in, then rose from his chair and came over and put his arms around her. There was no love in the gesture, nor sexuality, just warmth and thanks as he hugged her close then released her.

'It's a sweet suggestion, Julia, and I'm touched by it. But you mustn't worry your head about that call. I think I know why that person is making it, and in a way it's understandable.'

'You mean because they lost someone in that plane crash?' Julia said without thinking. Then, seeing his surprise, added quickly, 'Mrs Williamson mentioned it. She felt I should know.'

'Seems everyone in the company knows.' Rees returned to his chair and picked up his pen. 'Do me a favour and forget it. I've a deadline and can't waste my time talking about stupid threats.'

Sighing, Julia went to make him a cup of coffee and one for herself. After that call, she needed it. Strange how the reality of a situation differed from the way one imagined it would be. Her training as a Guardian had equipped her for most emergencies, and threatening calls had been part of it. But actually hearing a person utter a death threat in cold blood had made *her* blood run cold, and the lurid images she had had of Rees struggling, dying or dead, now held a grim reality.

She didn't blame him for being amused when she had offered to watch over him, for since meeting him she had done her best to hide her intelligence. Yet somehow she *had* to be with him night and day. His life was at stake, and guarding him her first priority.

If only she knew what he would say if she told him her true identity. Had she established a good enough relationship with him to do so? After all, he had made it plain he was attracted to her, and though she knew that this week he had seen Dawn as well as a rather ravishing redhead—having sat in her car with a headscarf and dark glasses as she followed him—she was sure that if she herself gave him any encouragement it would bring him straight back to her. But to do so would imply something she was not prepared to give, even in the interest of her job, which left her back at square one.

She took Rees' coffee into him, with two shortbreads as requested, and received an absent-minded thank you.

Rees at work had no time for flirtation, which pleased her, not only because it saved her tedious parrying, but because it showed a side of him she liked.

Sipping her coffee, she realised she had reached an impasse and needed Murray's advice. Making sure she wasn't overheard, she called him, deeply disappointed to learn he was still abroad. But, reflecting on it during the afternoon, she was rather glad she hadn't managed to contact him. Rees was her responsibility, and if she ran to Murray every time the going got tough he would interpret it as weakness, the last thing she wanted him to think of her. That being the case, she was still left with the million-dollar question of how to guard Rees at all times!

As if on cue, the door between them opened, and he stood on the threshold, stretching his arms above his head, and stifling a yawn. 'I'm packing it in for tonight. But you should have gone home ages ago. I told you I wouldn't need you.'

'I thought perhaps you might.'

'Can't bear to leave me, eh?' he teased.

'That's right,' she said, and, though it wasn't quite the truth, it wasn't that much of a lie either, for he looked so vulnerable standing there that she longed to go up and push away the fallen lock of hair from his brow, and smooth the lines from his face. His defences were down and she was seeing a side of him she hadn't seen before: the soft core behind the strength and genius. Startled by her thoughts, she hurriedly opened a drawer and pretended to search for something, so he wouldn't see her face.

'By the way,' he informed her, 'I'm flying to San Diego tomorrow.'

Startled, she looked up. 'That's rather sudden.'

'I know. But some of our new machinery is being installed in a factory there, and I want to inspect it for myself.'

'How long will you be away?'

'A few days.'

'I'm coming with you,' she said promptly. No way was she going to let Rees out her her sight. The assassin could be at the airport, on the aircraft, ready to strike at any time!

'Not that again,' Rees muttered. 'Much as I appreciate your concern, I assure you it's needless.'

'No, it isn't. Anyway, I've always wanted to see San Diego. I've heard it's a beautiful city. Please let me come with you, Rees.'

He shook his head, and in desperation she used her ace. 'It will give us a chance of being alone together. Wouldn't you like that?'

His eyebrows rose, dark silk lines above those arresting eyes of his, eyes which could spark with anger, grow frosty with disdain, gleam with amusement or glow with desire, but which she doubted had ever lit with love. For that was a word Rees didn't acknowledge. Not that he had ever said so, but his entire life-style—and he was already in his mid-thirties—indicated it.

'I hope you know what you're letting yourself in for,' he drawled. 'I'll be busy during the day, but there'll be the long evenings for you to entertain me.'

'Won't you be seeing business people and—and things like that?' she asked quickly.

'Not if you're with me.' The side of his mouth curved in a smile. 'If you want to change your mind, I'll understand.'

'No, I don't. I'm coming with you!'

'You've a kind heart, Julia,' he said unexpectedly.

'Why do you say that?'

'Because you've been keeping me at arm's length since we met, and now you're offering yourself to me on a plate! You're only willing to go to San Diego with me because you're worried for my safety.'

Julia took advantage of his perception, hoping that if she admitted he was right, it might keep him at bay. 'I just—I just don't want anything to happen to you,' she murmured.

'I don't want anything to happen to me, either! But as I said earlier, you're taking that call too seriously.'

'And you're not taking it seriously enough. So if you don't mind, I *will* come with you.' She took the bull by the horns. 'And I'll stay around tonight until you go back home. Unless you've a date with Dawn?'

'How do you know I've been seeing her?'

Caught out, Julia improvised wildly. 'Well, you've left *me* alone, so I assumed you were still dating her.'

'I've no date with anyone tonight,' Rees grinned, 'so we'll have a quick meal and I'll hit the sack.'

'What time is your plane leaving for San Diego tomorrow?'

'Noon. Why?'

'Because I want to be on the same flight, if possible.'

'Are you sure you know what you're doing?'

'Yes.'

'OK, then.' He chucked her under the chin. 'But don't say I didn't warn you!'

'I can defend myself,' she asserted, and when he grinned even more broadly hoped she wouldn't have to resort to another of Murray's self-defence tricks to prove it!

Rees was as tired as he had said, and they had a quick meal at a new restaurant nearby—a French bistro that was surprisingly good, which had opened to serve the newly built houses and apartments.

'Five years from now Docklands will be a real community,' Rees said, as he heartily demolished a delicious *coq au vin*.

'It isn't the sort of place to bring up children,' Julia commented.

'Maybe not. But that makes it even more perfect for me. There'll be no brats squealing about the place.'

'Don't you like children?'

'In their place. And that will never be mine!'

She might have known, Julia thought gloomily. A man bent only on pleasuring himself wouldn't want the problems of marriage and raising a family, even if the problems could be smoothed over by his wealth.

'You don't hide your displeasure too well,' he teased, and she glanced up from her plate to see him watching her.

'I was thinking what a lonely old man you'll be.'

'I'm sure I'll always find someone to take care of me. And if I can't, I'll arrange for a couple of anonymous telephone calls and death threats!'

'Don't expect *me* to come running,' Julia said pertly. 'By then I'll be living in a rose-covered cottage with a doting husband and grandchildren around me.'

'All women are the same,' Rees grumbled. 'They can't think of love without commitment. It must be bred in their bones. Even the majority of feminists ease up on their convictions when they get to their late thirties.'

He was deliberately laying himself open to argument, but Julia knew better than to rise to the bait. Had she been dining with him on a purely social basis, she would have had no hesitation in cutting his comments to shreds. But, since it was her duty to make herself desirable and necessary to him, she swallowed her chagrin.

After dinner, she made no demur when he headed for his apartment. However, once in the foyer, she stopped and asked the porter to get her a cab.

Rees made no effort to hide his amusement. 'Come up for a drink first, and I'll drive you home myself.'

'No. That man might be lurking outside. I'll feel happier if I know you're safe in your apartment.'

'But *you* don't feel safe there!'

'Should I?'

'Definitely not.' Rees hesitated. 'So think twice about San Diego!'

'I'll feel differently there,' she lied. 'In England I'm more—more inhibited.'

Rees's reply was cut short by the arrival of a cab depositing another resident, and Julia rushed to tell the driver to wait, then insisted on going up with Rees to his apartment and waiting while he unlocked his front door and switched off the alarm system.

'Don't forget to put it on again before you go to sleep,' she cautioned.

'You really take these threats seriously, don't you?'

'Because I'm sensible. And it's a pity *you* aren't.'

'I'll be very sensible tonight,' he assured her. 'I don't want to die before our trip to America!'

Ignoring this, Julia blew him a kiss, and headed back to the foyer.

'Julia,' Rees called, and she paused and glanced back. 'I understand your fear for my safety,' he said softly, 'but I'm perfectly capable of looking after myself, and I don't like possessive women.'

'I don't want to possess you,' she said sweetly. 'Only to make sure you're alive and well.'

'And able to perform?' he enquired silkily. 'I promise you won't have any complaints on that score!'

Colour flooded her face and, furious with herself, Julia stepped into the elevator, Rees' laughter ringing in her ears. Drat the man! San Diego looked like becoming their battleground, and she had to steel herself for it. Rees had endless charm and was ruthless enough to use it to his advantage. But she could be ruthless too, and when it came to her emotional safety she knew how to put up the barricades.

Only when she was in her own living-room did she slump in a chair and relax. One more night safely over. Maybe when this job was finished she would settle for another sheika! It would certainly be less wearing on her nerves.

The purr of the telephone had her reaching for it, and she was delighted to hear Murray's voice.

'I've just flown in from Rome and heard you were trying to contact me,' he said. 'How are things?'

Concisely she filled him in, aware of his interest quickening when she told him of the telephone call she had listened into earlier that evening, and that she had persuaded Rees to take her with him to San Diego.

'You'll still be faced with the same problems when you get back,' Murray stated, 'unless you move in with him, of course. If Denton weren't so pig-headed, this whole ridiculous charade could be avoided.'

'I know. But I'm managing to cope, though I've had a few nerve-racking moments.'

'Oh?' Murray's tone was interested. 'Care to fill me in?'

'Not particularly,' she chuckled, 'but I will. Rees has his pick of adoring females, but at the moment seems intent on picking *me*.'

'That's what we planned on,' Murray reminded her. 'But don't do anything you don't want to.'

'I won't,' she said drily. 'Anxious as I am to protect our client, I'd rather be a store detective than go against my principles.'

'There won't be any more store work for you,' Murray said crisply. 'I've had a letter from Sir Andrew, singing your praises, and from now on you'll be up front with the men.'

'Honestly?'

'Absolutely.'

'That's the best news you could have given me,' she said happily. 'I can't wait till this job's over. Much more of Rees Denton, and *I* might end up as his assassin!'

CHAPTER SIX

JULIA was so delighted she had managed to talk Rees into letting her accompany him to the States that she barely slept the night, and was so tired next day that she dozed for most of the flight. Not that this seemed to bother Rees, for he was absorbed with a stack of documents and only woke her as they came in to land.

It was early evening when they arrived, having flown over the Pole to Los Angeles, where they had changed planes.

As she had anticipated, it was a beautiful city, with wonderful homes set in the hills high above it, and equally wonderful ones ranged along the shore, with a view of the tossing blue-grey Pacific Ocean. There was always a faint breeze here to lessen the heat, and it blew soft tendrils of hair across Julia's face as they drove from the airport to their hotel.

She had hoped they would be staying in one with a sea view, but found it to be in the heart of the city itself, though it was set in beautiful gardens where fountains shimmered among the palms and oriental shrubs.

But she hadn't come here to appreciate the views, the climate or the buildings, only to safeguard the dynamic man beside her. No easy task, she suspected with dismay as they entered a lobby teeming with people. But she was happy to see they had been booked into a suite, both their bedrooms opening into a charmingly furnished sitting-room. When she had called the hotel yesterday to say she was coming, she had asked for a bedroom next door to Rees', and wondered whether *he* had made another call to request the suite. But she was not about to look a gift horse in the mouth, and she accepted the change of accommodation without comment.

She was unpacking her case when she felt herself being watched, and looked up to see Rees lounging against the doorjamb. He had discarded his jacket and shirt, and she saw his broad shoulders owed nothing to his tailor. Although he was a swarthy man, his dark skin had a golden glow. Sun-kissed, she thought, and had a sudden desire to touch his silk-textured skin.

Watch it! she warned herself. This man can be dangerous to your peace of mind. On the other hand, one of the reasons she had changed jobs had been in the hope of meeting someone she would like, and there was no point pretending she didn't like Rees. In fact, it was a liking that could grow into something deeper. But she dared not allow it, for he had his future cut and dried, and it didn't include any of the things she held dear.

'If you aren't too tired,' he said, 'we can go out to dinner. There's a wonderful restaurant in——'

'Let's dine here,' she cut in, thinking it safer.

He knew the reason instantly, and went to argue. But she looked at him meltingly and had the pleasure of watching him nod agreement.

What a powerful weapon physical attraction was, she thought soberly, as she showered and dressed. It made the strongest person weak, and the weakest strong. It gave hope, and it could equally cause despair. Yes, like most emotions it had a good and a bad side, and had to be treated with respect and caution.

Rees was waiting in the sitting-room when she came in, the sensuous movement of his lower lip showing he was not unmoved by the lovely picture she made. Beautiful, no matter what she wore, she was breathtaking at her best, and tonight she was definitely at her best, her white crêpe dress skimming her body and barely hinting at the curves beneath, yet somehow making one intensely conscious of them as she sauntered forward in her best model-girl walk.

'You look perfect,' Rees said huskily, breathing in the scent of her as she stopped in front of him. 'So perfect, I'm almost afraid to touch you in case I find you're only a dream.'

Oh, lord! she thought. And this was *before* dinner!

'You look pretty good yourself,' she replied, and he certainly did. His silver-grey suit of some thin silk material was as superbly tailored as his business clothes. Yet it had a casualness about it that spoke of the best Italian tailoring. It really was a pity he was intent on staying single.

All eyes were riveted to them as they entered the hotel dining-room—the women to Rees, the men to her—and though Rees, no slouch when it came to taking out a lovely girl, must be used to having his dates admired, he seemed vaguely irritated by the stir she caused.

'If that guy at the next table doesn't stop staring at you, I'll punch him on the jaw!'

'You wouldn't,' she said quickly.

'No, I wouldn't,' he agreed with the faintest of smiles, 'but I do find it annoying.'

'Doesn't it make you feel good to know your choice of companion is admired?' she asked with genuine curiosity.

'I already know I have excellent taste in women, and I don't like us being the centre of attraction. It cramps my style.'

'I haven't noticed,' she teased. 'You're doing very well.'

'I'll do better when we're alone.' He reached under the table and placed his hand on her thigh.

She forced herself not to tense, and was not sure quite what she would do if his hand travelled to a more intimate place. But in this she had misjudged him, for, though she knew Rees to be a wolf, he was a wolf only in his lair, and he withdrew his hand almost immediately, making her realise it was merely a gesture of intent.

But it was an intent not to be ignored, and it almost made her chicken out from what she had to do. Yet what price a passionate clinch or two if it helped save Rees' life? Surely that was more important than... But she dared not finish the question, and to keep it at bay she stood up and drew Rees on to the floor.

An excellent combo was playing languorous music, and he took advantage of it to hold her close, his hands curving her body into his as they moved slowly in time to the beat.

'If I didn't know you better,' he murmured, 'I'd say you were trying to seduce me.'

'I'm coming between you and a bullet,' she retorted.

He laughed. 'For the first time I'm grateful to this madman. Without him, I'd never have got you here.'

'Don't count your chickens.'

'Why not? Anticipation can be as good as the feast.'

Anticipation is all you're going to get, she thought mutinously, and decided there was nothing more irritating to a woman than an over-confident man. But then, why shouldn't he be over-confident when his little black book was bulging with names?

'I'm hungry,' she said, pulling away from him and leading him back to the table.

'Me, too,' he replied. 'How about oysters or caviare? Both are excellent aphrodisiacs.'

'Oh, dear,' she said in a puzzled voice. 'I didn't know you were in need of it.'

Thinking she was teasing him, he started to smile; then, seeing her face—which with a supreme effort she kept serious—he looked dumbstruck.

'I certainly *don't* need it,' he declared. 'I was being funny.'

'You've an odd sense of humour, then.' She saw him bite back a retort, and knew her stupidity was annoying him. All to the good. She was only beginning! Unthinkingly, she reached for her wine-glass.

'I thought you don't drink?' Rees commented, alert as ever.

'I don't normally. It's just the excitement of being abroad.'

'Don't tell me this is your first time?'

'Apart from a day trip to Paris,' she lied, forgetting Rome and New York and Tokyo where she had gone to be photographed for the front covers of *Harpers* and *Vogue*.

'You seem to have lead an extremely sheltered life for a very beautiful girl.'

'Beautiful girls have to be careful,' she said primly. 'I don't want to end up on the white slave market.'

Rees choked on his drink and she made a sympathetic sound. 'Did it go down the wrong way?'

'No—yes!'

Biting her lip to stop herself laughing, she studied the menu with rapt attention, then gave her order.

Their talk during the meal was desultory, and Julia uttered so many boring platitudes she was hard pressed not to yawn. Rees manfully did his best to guide the conversation, but she wasn't having it, and led everything back to her favourite topics: clothes and film stars.

'What did you do before you came to work for me?' Rees asked, in desperation to stem her saga of how she had tried to form a fan club for Tom Cruise.

He had asked the same question when he had first interviewed her, but she had avoided answering. Now, however, she was obliged to.

'I was a photographic model.'

'Really?' His mouth curved upwards. 'I have a vague recollection of you telling me all models were witless!'

Vague, was he? He seemed to have total recall!

'Then I was in the right profession, wasn't I?' she giggled.

On the verge of nodding, he stopped himself, and she awarded him full marks for control. Intent on making love to her, it would hardly be diplomatic of him to agree.

'Surely you've done *some* office work?' he ventured. 'Otherwise Mrs Williamson wouldn't have recommended you.'

'Aren't I a good personal assistant?' Julia countered.

'You're excellent.'

'Then that's why she chose me. She knew I was fed up modelling and wanted to try my hand at something else.'

'What will you do when Mrs Williamson returns?'

'I haven't thought that far. Maybe you can find a niche for me.'

'There's a glass alcove beside my bed!'

She laughed, her head tilting, and his eyes went swiftly to the creamy curve of her throat.

'You've a lovely laugh, Julia, and a lovely voice too. So many girls haven't.'

Giving him a sibylline smile, she said nothing, and was not sorry when he signed the bill and rose, for it was heaven knew what time in the morning on *her* body clock, though Rees seemed totally unconcerned by jet lag.

'Don't you ever get tired?' she asked as they walked down the corridor towards their suite.

'Not when I'm doing something I like,' he smiled, unlocking the door, 'and I like being with you.'

She walked swiftly ahead of him across the sitting-room. 'Will you forgive me if I go straight to bed? I'm too tired to talk any more.'

'Who wants to talk?' He followed her into her bedroom, and closed the door.

She swung round. 'I don't remember inviting you in.'

'There's invitation in every inch of you.' He reached for her and, before she could protest, her mouth was taken by his.

As always, his gentleness surprised her, disarmed her too. Had he grasped her with rough passion, she would have fought him off, and in the doing quelled her desire. But his gentleness was her *undoing*, and she found herself responding to him. Physically he was everything she wanted in a man. Mentally too, for he was intelligent, humorous, brilliant in his profession and full of common sense—except where he himself was concerned! Unfortunately he was also a womaniser, which was a big black mark against him; and, forcibly reminding herself she didn't want to be another name in it, she tried to push him away.

Rees would have none of it; keeping his mouth firmly on hers, he skilfully unzipped her dress. The white sliver of crêpe slithered to the ground, leaving her body covered only by white lace panties. She tried to escape his hold, but his hands were too firm and, lifting her off her feet, he carried her to the bed.

'No!' she protested. 'Let me go.'

Paying no attention to her pleas, he came down beside her, lying half across her body and pinning her to the bed with his weight. As his eyes took in her near nakedness, a flame sparked in their dark depths, growing in intensity as they roamed her firm breasts, surprisingly full for such a slender body. The nipples were large, aureoled by pink, their colour deepening as his hands cupped the fullness, and lean fingers began a subtle caress.

Julia knew she should fight him, but found it impossible when he was arousing such a multitude of wonderful emotions in her, emotions she had never experienced with anyone else. She had been kissed and touched before, though not touched so intimately, and she was trembling with a desire stronger than she had ever imagined herself capable of feeling.

I must push him away, she thought, but not yet, not yet...

Her hands lightly skimmed his shoulders, and at her touch he muttered deep in his throat. She didn't know when he had removed his shirt, all she knew was that she wanted an even greater intimacy. And so did he, for his lips left hers and traced a path of fire from her breasts to her navel, then lower still, his hands pushing aside the wisp of lace to find the softness of her inner thighs and the hot bud throbbing there.

Even as his mouth sought it, her sanity returned, and with a superhuman effort she pushed him away and wriggled free.

'Darling, don't.' He reached for her again.

'No!' she cried. 'I can't.' Yet she knew that if she remained close to him she would, and that if she did, she would be going against her long-held belief of giving herself only to the man she would marry. And Rees would as soon as marry as go to prison!

Instantly she saw her solution. What an idiot she was not to have thought of it before. Brain racing like a souped-up sports car, she clutched his shoulders and pulled him down upon her.

Startled, his eyes stared into hers; then, deciding to accept her change of heart and take what she was now offering, he began raining kisses over her face.

'I love you so much,' she whispered in a breathless, little-girl voice.

'You're beautiful,' he replied. 'I never realised, never knew...'

'We'll be so happy together, darling,' she cooed into his ear. 'I can't wait till we're married.'

If she had flung a bucket of cold water over him, he couldn't have reacted more violently. His hands dropped from her body as if it were a hot coal, and he sat up straight.

'Married? Who said anything about marriage?'

'But you—I thought...' Julia widened her eyes at him. 'But you want to go to bed with me, don't you?'

'What the hell has that to do with marriage?' Rees jumped off the bed as if it were on fire, and glared at her. 'I can't believe I'm hearing straight. You're not serious, are you?'

'Of course I'm serious.' Julia made her voice wobble pathetically. 'But it s-seems *you* aren't. I'm s-sorry I misunderstood you.'

'So am I.' Belatedly aware of the tremor in her voice, Rees' own grew gentler. 'I never believed that in this day and age a sophisticated girl would regard going to bed with someone as a proposal of marriage.'

'I've never pretended to be sophisticated,' Julia gulped, enjoying herself so much she didn't mind prolonging this conversation, and awarding herself a gold medal for having come up with this fantastic idea. 'I've always told you I'm old-fashioned.'

'You're archaic!' he retorted.

Her violet eyes lifted to his as she carefully covered herself with a silk sheet. 'But I love you, Rees, and I thought you loved me.'

He went to speak but seemed to find it impossible, and Julia decided not to give him time to find a way out of a situation she intended to use to her advantage. Yet not just to *her* advantage, but to his too, for what she now planned would enable her to stick as close to him as glue to a stamp.

'Maybe we shouldn't be in such a hurry,' she went on. 'Maybe we should try it out first.'

'Try what out first?'

'Living together.'

'*Living* together?' His tone was incredulous.

'To see if we're compatible.' She hung her head as if in embarrassment. 'I don't mean compatible in bed. That must wait until we're quite sure we're right for each other. But first we must make sure we get on in every other way.'

'Get on?' Rees still looked bemused.

'That's what I said.' Julia dared not meet his eyes for fear of laughing. 'We'll have a purely platonic relationship. Almost the real thing, but not quite.'

'"Not quite" being the operative words,' he muttered.

'Don't be angry with me, Rees,' she pleaded.

'I'm not. I'm astonished.' He shook his head. 'Just when I think I'm getting to know you, I find I don't.'

'That's all to the good,' she beamed. 'It means I'll never bore you.'

'That's for sure,' he said drily. 'In fact, keeping up with the way your mind works is a full-time occupation, and highly exhausting.'

'You're exhausted because of jet lag.' Julia bounced off the bed, still clutching the sheet around her. 'Goodnight, Rees darling. Sleep well.'

'I'd have slept better with *you*,' he said wryly, and went out.

Alone, Julia danced a little jig, only stopping when she stumbled over the sheet. She would never forget the look on Rees' face when she had pretended she had thought he wanted to marry her. If only there had been a hidden camera in the room! Still, he had played into her hands and made her job much easier, for which she was highly delighted!

CHAPTER SEVEN

DETERMINED not to oversleep, Julia set her alarm, and was waiting in the sitting-room, showered and dressed, when Rees entered it at eight-thirty.

He stopped in surprise at sight of her. 'Why are you up so early?'

'To go with you to your meeting.'

'I don't need an assistant with me.'

'I didn't come here for that reason,' she stated matter-of-factly. 'I came to protect you.'

He burst out laughing. 'You? You couldn't protect a butterfly.'

'You're right. They're too easy to catch. But the madman that's threatening to kill you might be waiting in the corridor. Or outside the hotel.'

'That's not logical,' Rees said impatiently. 'We're pretty sure he's British, and he's hardly likely to kill me in a strange country, where he would be far more noticeable. In fact, I don't know why I didn't think of it yesterday and stopped you coming with me.'

'Because you wanted to get me into bed, and thought you'd stand a better chance here.'

Rees had the grace to colour. 'Honesty must be your middle name.'

'It was nearly my first name,' she said ingenuously. 'My mother's a keen gardener, and she says honesty is a lovely flower.' Head on one side, Julia appraised him. 'I wonder what she'd have christened you?'

'A garden implement,' Rees said wryly. 'Something like a rake!'

Julia's laugh was genuine, though so far this morning none of her conversation had been. But it was fun playing Miss Dumb-bell, provided she managed to get in a few digs at this Lothario, who had brought her here for the sole purpose of seducing her. She fumed at the very idea, then firmly pushed the thought aside, remembering Murray's dictum never to let personalities come between her and her work.

For the next two days Julia did not leave Rees' side, though several times during their first morning together he had tried to persuade her to go sightseeing and enjoy herself.

But she would have none of it, and after a second try Rees gave up on her, and with ill-concealed irritation accepted her presence, though he insisted she tell no one that his life had been threatened.

Julia had never seen Rees with his managing director's hat, for in London he was more the inventor-cum-engineer. But during these few days he met with the heads of various large companies and showed a grasp of complex financial matters that left her reeling in admiration.

On their second and third nights, Rees had business dinners, but luckily as his PA she was included in them, though he did his best to ignore her. Since their discussion in her bedroom, he had remained strictly impersonal, and each night when they returned to their suite he went directly to his room. She had a vague suspicion he even locked his door!

Although she was happy to go along with his behaviour for the moment, it made no difference to her master plan which she intended putting into action the moment they returned to London. One day, when she had stopped working for Guardians, this entire episode was going to make a marvellous after-dinner story!

Their departure was delayed by an unexpected order for more of Rees's grey boxes, and it wasn't until the following Sunday, seven days after leaving Heathrow, that they returned to it. A car was waiting to meet them and, recognising the chauffeur as another Guardian employee, Julia was content to let Rees drop her off at her apartment first.

He bade her a curt good morning and said he would see her in the office on Monday and, watching the back of his dark head as he was driven away, she could sympathise with his frustration. She had alternately blown hot and cold with him, and though she had reached the peak of infuriating behaviour in San Diego he had taken it like a man. An annoyed one, admittedly, but one with sufficient control not to try to coerce her into changing her mind. But then, why should he? As he had once said, he had never found there to be a shortage of willing women.

No sooner had she unpacked than she called Murray and outlined her new strategy.

'Wish I could see Denton's face when you confront him,' he said when he had stopped laughing. 'Keep me posted on what happens.'

Smiling with anticipation, Julia went to the cupboard for a larger suitcase and began packing all over again, at the same time working out the story she was going to spin Rees.

An hour later, two cases at her feet, she was ringing his doorbell. There was no answer, and she grew nervous. The porter on duty had assured her Mr Denton was in, and had only allowed her into the penthouse elevator because he recognised her. So why wasn't Rees answering? She rang again and was wondering whether she dare pick the lock and run the risk of setting off the alarm, when the door was flung open by an irate Rees, his skin glistening damply, his body partially covered by a short, navy towelling robe.

'You!' he exclaimed, then saw the cases. 'What the——'

'It's the best way,' she cut across him.

'Best way to what?'

'To see if we're compatible. That's why I'm moving in with you.'

'Moving in with me? *Here?*' Surprise gave way to astonishment. 'I don't remember asking you.'

'Not in so many words,' she agreed, keeping a smile clamped to her mouth. 'But you implied it, didn't you? The night you came into my room and undressed me.'

'You can't be serious!' He tightened the belt of his robe, but not before she had caught a glimpse of a muscular thigh lightly flecked with dark hair. 'Look, Julia, I'm afraid you misunderstood my intentions. You're a lovely girl and I—well, I fancied you like mad. But there was nothing more to it than that. As I've already made plain to you, I have no intention of *ever* marrying.'

'But I thought you loved me.' Julia puckered her face, but could not manage to squeeze any tears from her eyes, though she screwed them up tightly. 'You couldn't have kissed me the way you did if you didn't feel something for me.'

'I could have done a lot more than kiss you without being in love with you,' he snorted. 'Dammit, this is the nineteen eighties, not the eighteen eighties! Now, be a good girl and go home. If you wait till I change, I'll drive you back.'

'I can't go back.' She launched into her prepared story. 'When I walked into the apartment this morning I found Mrs Elton there. The owner,' she explained. 'The woman

I was house-sitting for. She wasn't due back for several months, but her plans changed and—and she doesn't need me any more.'

Rees' mouth set in a tight line. 'She can't throw you out. Didn't she engage you for a specific length of time?'

'No. She said she would be away three months, but we didn't bother about a contract.' Seeing no softening of Rees' expression, Julia played her trump card. 'I think one of the neighbours must have written and told her I'd left the apartment—when I went with you to San Diego. That's probably why she came back and was so horrid to me.'

'Didn't you tell her *why* you came with me?' Rees demanded. 'I know it was misguided of you, but you did it with the best of intentions. Would you like me to have a word with her?'

'It won't do any good. She's terribly obstinate.'

'Like some others I know,' Rees muttered.

'Anyway, I think it was fated to happen. I'm sure I'm meant to stay here instead, so I told her I was quite happy to go because I was moving in with my fiancé.'

'You *what*?'

'I see now that it was a mistake,' Julia snivelled, 'and I'm sorry for not realising you were only amusing yourself with me.'

This time she managed to squeeze out some tears, though they were tears of rage when she thought how fast and loose he played with women, and what pleasure it would be to give him his come-uppance at the same time that she was guarding him. It would make her job doubly worth while!

'Don't cry,' Rees said curtly. 'That's a woman's favourite weapon.'

'I haven't any weapons to use against you.' Julia cried harder. 'But I've nowhere to go—and—and I came here because I thought you loved me.'

'Don't you have any friends?'

'None I can stay with.'

'Why not move into a hotel until you find yourself an apartment, or another house-sitting job?'

'Those sort of jobs aren't easy to come by. And it might take me weeks.' She raised tear-drenched eyes to his, her long lashes glittering with moisture. 'Can't I stay here for a little while, Rees? Now I know you don't love me, I promise I'll keep out of your way as much as possible.'

He looked as if he were about to refuse, and she held her breath, realising that if he said 'no', she would have no choice but to go. But she was counting on his not being as hard-bitten as he sounded, and when he gave a heavy sigh and reached out for her cases she knew she was right.

'Just till you find somewhere else,' he stated.

'Oh, thank you,' she breathed tremulously, and followed him down the marble-floored corridor into a beautifully appointed bedroom with its own small terrace and breathtaking view of the Thames and London beyond it.

'What a lovely room!' she exclaimed, genuinely delighted to find it less starkly modern than the rest of the apartment, with hand-painted French furniture, a delicately sprigged carpet in pale green and pink, and matching curtains and duvet.

'This isn't a bit like the rest of your home,' she couldn't help saying.

'It came from my father's house,' he said curtly, the set of his mouth precluding her from further comment or questions.

'You have your own bathroom,' he went on, pointing to a door behind her. 'And if there's anything you require, ask my housekeeper. She comes in on a daily basis.'

'I can't see myself needing anything,' Julia smiled, and spun round on her heel. Her full skirt lifted, giving him a better view of her shapely legs, and seeing the way his eyes went instantly to them she said firmly, 'No funny tricks, Rees. Now I know you don't love me, my staying here is purely a platonic arrangement.'

'Most definitely,' he agreed, and stalked out.

Julia tiptoed to the door and inched it open to watch him return to his bedroom. A moment later she heard his shower come on. Only then did she call Murray.

'I never thought you'd get away with it,' he chuckled.

'Nor did I, to be honest. He put up a fight to begin with, and then sort of caved in.'

'He was probably scared you'd make a scene or start telling everyone he'd tried to seduce you.'

'I'd never have done that.' Julia was shocked.

'*You* wouldn't,' Murray said, 'but the character you're playing might well have done, and he could have found himself getting some unwanted publicity.'

'You think that would have worried him?'

'Not in the normal course of events, but I had a word with Sir Andrew after you called me earlier—I thought I should put him in the picture—and he told me that as of now, Rees is going to be Mr Whiter than White in order to clinch a fantastic deal with Bargett Engineering. Seems that Bargett himself is devoutly religious, and won't do business with anyone whose lifestyle he disapproves of. Hence Rees being careful not to step out of line until contracts have been exchanged.'

So *that* accounted for his easy capitulation! Julia thought wryly, and here she was thinking he had taken pity on her! Still, it had given her the 'in' she required, so who was she to complain? But once he had signed the contract, she would be out on her ear. If only the police could find the assassin before then!

'I appreciate the way you've put your heart into this assignment,' Murray said into the silence. 'No male security guard could have done what you have.'

Julia couldn't help laughing. 'Certainly not with a womaniser like Rees!'

'He's no worse than most bachelors of his age and position. You're too tough on him.'

'I don't think so.' Julia's cool tones were quickly picked up by Murray.

'OK, so you're telling me to mind my own business.'

'No, I'm not. But you're a bachelor too and you're bound to defend Rees.'

On a note of laughter the call ended, and as she unpacked and placed her clothes in the capacious wardrobe she reflected on what Murray had said. Her four brothers, good-looking all, had played the field as hard as Rees, but the three who were now married had proved themselves ideal husbands. Except that Rees wasn't interested in changing his single status.

She tried envisaging him as a husband, coming home each night to talk over the events of the day with his wife, to share a meal, maybe help stack the dishes in the dishwasher. All the hundred and one mundane chores that went to make up a life together. She shook her head. Rees would never fit into that kind of picture. He was a love 'em and leave 'em type, ready to forget the old when someone new appeared. But would a girl who had been loved by Rees forget *him*?

Disturbed at where her thoughts had taken her, Julia clamped down on them. Falling for Rees was the last thing she wanted. She would as soon fall for a boa constrictor!

Julia settled into Rees' apartment more easily than she had anticipated. She left for work with him in the morning and returned with him in the evening, the two occasions when he was most at risk. For the first few evenings he had worked late at the office and been too tired to go out socially afterwards. Which was all to the good as far as she was concerned.

It was only when he remained home for the fourth and fifth evening that the penny dropped. Of course! Rees intended leading an exemplary life until the deal he was working on was completed and signed. No wonder the telephone numbers in his little black book remained unrung, and he was content to eat the dinners Mrs Hartley left prepared for him, before she departed each afternoon at five.

Julia, careful to keep out of his way once they were home, prepared herself a quick snack and ate it in the kitchen, closing her senses to the delicious smells wafting from the dining-room where Rees was enjoying the cordon bleu dishes which he had only to heat in the microwave.

It wasn't until the end of the week that she suddenly wondered if Rees had given any thought to the possibility that Mr Bargett might discover he was sharing his home with his assistant, who happened to be a rather comely young female.

However, she had no intention of asking him, and was smiling to herself when he strolled into the kitchen as she was making a sandwich, and brusquely told her Mrs Hartley had prepared enough dinner for two.

'Unless you prefer sandwiches,' he finished, glancing at the bread and cheese in her hand.

'What are you offering instead?'

'Veal cutlet in asparagus creamed sauce, gratin potatoes and fresh broccoli, followed by peach pie.'

'That's an offer I can't refuse.' Julia whisked the bread back into the bin and the cheese into the refrigerator, and nipped smartly ahead of Rees into the dining-room.

Eating at the glass and steel table, with Rees opposite her, and behind him the glorious panorama of London, she wondered what it would be like to be married to this man. Physically exciting, as she knew to her cost, mentally stimulating too, but emotionally barren, for Rees was basically a loner.

She found herself curious to know something of his background, but did not see him taking kindly to being cross-questioned, and wondered if Murray knew anything about him. Yet she wouldn't ask Murray either, for he was a perceptive man and she didn't want him assuming she had any feeling for Rees other than on a purely professional basis.

After all, when the person threatening him was caught, she would step out of his life and never see him again. The knowledge should have delighted her, yet it didn't, and pondering why, she admitted that in an odd way she had grown to like him—inasmuch as it was possible to like a man who regarded women only as sex objects.

That evening set the scene for the next week. Julia would re-heat the dinner Mrs Hartley had prepared, and she and Rees then ate together, sometimes in the dining-room, sometimes in the more intimate atmosphere of the kitchen, if black granite worktops and steel cabinets and fittings could be called intimate. It was more like an operating theatre, Julia thought as she took a bowl of fluffy white rice out of the microwave and set it on the table, its shape following the unusual bow window that formed a dining nook.

'Seen any suitable accommodation for yourself?' Rees asked, taking a bottle of Chablis from the refrigerator.

'Heaps. But nothing affordable.'

'I'll give you a raise.' He filled her glass and his own, then motioned her to help herself to the chicken casserole.

'It won't do much good once Mrs Williamson comes back and I'm looking for another job.'

'You shouldn't have difficulty finding one. You're an excellent assistant. Quick, efficient and with plenty of initiative.'

Julia hid a grin. The last part was certainly true! 'So I take it you'll give me a good reference?'

'You can write it yourself, and bring it in for me to sign.'

'That would be dishonest,' she said in shocked tones.

He grunted and heaped his plate high. 'Mmm, this smells good. If you'd like Mrs Hartley to prepare something special for the weekend, by all means tell her.'

'I rather fancy lobster salad for Sunday lunch. Unless you'll be out?'

'I'm staying home for the next few weeks,' came the firm answer.

Julia waited for him to explain why, and was not surprised when he didn't. Even Rees, cynic that he was, was not going to admit he was playing a part in order to clinch a business contract.

'Of course, if you'd like to cook something yourself,' he went on, 'I've no objection.'

'I'm quite happy for Mrs Hartley to do it.'

'But don't you *enjoy* cooking?' he persisted. 'I've been told this is a fabulous kitchen to work in.'

'I'm sure it is—if you like working in kitchens. But I don't.'

'You *can* cook, though?' he ventured. 'I mean, if you had to, you could whip up something delicious?'

'Nutritious,' Julia corrected. 'I doubt it would be delicious. My soufflés fall flat, likewise my sponge cakes; my pastry is hard as a brick, and my omelettes are fine for soling shoes.'

Rees raised a silky, black eyebrow. 'I'm amazed you don't mind admitting it.'

Only then did it dawn on Julia that she had been answering out of character. Well, out of character to the ingenuous 'I'll only go to bed with the man I marry' girl she was pretending to be, but very much in character with her real self. But it was too late to backtrack, and she had to plough on as best she could.

'I suppose all your ladyfriends are great cooks in between their busy career-girl lives?'

'They are, as it so happens. Most of them love cooking.'

'Because they see it as a way to a man's heart. Even in this day and age. But I'd never pretend to be what I'm not.' Julia could not cross her fingers for they were holding her knife and fork, so she crossed her legs instead. 'But when I marry I'm sure I'll be good around the house.'

'As long as you're good in the bedroom, don't worry!' Rees grinned wolfishly, and Julia promptly put down her fork.

'That's not funny.'

'Too right. I was serious. If a man finds a woman compatible with him in bed, he'll accept her being a poor housekeeper.'

'Would you?' Julia questioned sweetly.

'I wasn't talking personally,' Rees said. 'As you know, I'm not interested in marriage. Which is why I asked whether you've found some place else to live. The sooner you leave here, the sooner you'll forget me and start making another life for yourself.'

Julia longed to throw a plate at him. Conceited swine! Yet she could hardly blame him when she had appeared on his doorstep, cases in hand, ready for a platonic trial marriage.

'There's no point making another social life for myself while I'm seeing you every day in the office. But once Mrs Williamson is back and I can leave you, I'll be able to forget you.' She picked up her fork and resumed eating, stopping as she became aware of Rees watching her intently.

'Anything wrong?' she asked.

He shrugged. 'Unrequited love hasn't affected your appetite.'

She swallowed hastily. 'I think I'm getting over you. There's nothing like living with a man for opening your eyes to his faults.'

'Indeed?' Rees' voice was dry. 'And what faults have you suddenly discovered in me?'

Ready for the question, Julia returned her answer as fast as Steffi Graff a poor serve. 'You're impatient, untidy, tetchy in the morning until you've had your coffee, and generally short-tempered after midnight.'

'That's because living like a monk goes against my temperament. God, if this contract——' He stopped, and she reached for her wine-glass and pretended she had not heard.

Lying in bed that night, she knew Rees couldn't continue this celibate existence much longer, and was not surprised when, at six next evening, he announced he was leaving the office and going out to dinner.

Would it be with Dawn, she wondered, or the gorgeous redhead whose name she had still not discovered? Or maybe the elf-like brunette he had dated three times in succession before they had gone to the States? But whichever, he would soon be off with the old and on with the new, for he saw safety in numbers.

Sitting beside him as they drove home, she wished he was not going out tonight. She enjoyed their evenings together, particularly since he was treating her as a friend, careful to say nothing which she could construe as another proposal of marriage! Yet he was not a man to whom aloofness with the opposite sex came easily. He was very tactile, and frequently put a hand on her arm or across her shoulders. Nor could he help appraising her each morning when she came out of her room, his varying expressions showing quite clearly whether or not he approved of her outfit. Indeed, he was knowledgeable about women's fashions, and she found herself dressing to please him, liking it when his eyes lit with appreciation.

As soon as they entered the apartment, he disappeared into his bedroom and she went into hers, changed into a tracksuit and made for the kitchen and a cup of coffee, debating whether to trail Rees herself tonight or see if Murray had someone free to do it. She heard the telephone tinkle several times, and after the fourth occasion he appeared at the kitchen door, his expression distinctly irritable.

'No one's free,' he said abruptly. 'There's some big charity ball on tonight, and they all seem to be going to it.'

'Poor Rees,' Julia commiserated falsely. 'You shouldn't have left it so late before ringing.'

'I've never had this trouble before.'

'Well, we're all getting older,' she said brightly, and seeing his eyes spark with temper, added, 'At least the girls are, and they probably don't like sitting around waiting till you deign to call.'

'There's no deign about it,' came the curt response. 'I often don't know until the last moment if I'll be free.'

'*I* wouldn't hang around waiting for a man to call me.'

'Not even me?'

'*Especially* you.'

'You fall out of love fast, don't you?' he sneered.

'Maybe I was never in love with you. All I know is I——' She stopped and looked down demurely. 'I'm still very fond of you, but—but in a sisterly way.'

'That's all I need,' he groaned.

'You should be pleased. When you thought I wanted to marry you, you got in a dreadful panic.'

'Because I didn't want you to be hurt,' he came back at her quickly, 'and I'm delighted to hear you aren't. Though I must say I didn't think your emotions were so shallow.'

Julia's temper rose. 'Would you have been happier if I'd pined for you for ever?'

'Don't be silly.'

'Then why are you cross because I'm not?'

'I'm not in the least cross,' he said between gritted teeth. 'Now, for God's sake go and get ready.'

'Ready for what?'

'Dinner at the Ritz.' He waited for her to look pleased, and when she didn't, said sharply, 'What's wrong now?'

'I don't like being a last resort.'

He opened his mouth to say she was not, then obviously thought better of it. 'You're a beautiful girl, Julia, as I've told you many times before, and I would be delighted to be seen with you.'

'Even though you think me silly and naïve?'

'You're not always silly and naïve. Only sometimes. But we're getting away from the point. I didn't think of asking you out because I wasn't sure you'd want to come with me now you've decided you don't love me.'

'You don't have to be in love with someone to go out to dinner with them,' Julia said as if she were speaking to a child. 'After all, *you* don't love me, yet you're asking me out.'

The logic of her comment made him roll his eyes heavenwards, and stifling her laughter she walked out of the kitchen.

'Where are you going?' he called.

'To change, of course. You wouldn't want me to go out with you in a tracksuit!'

Sensing this might be their last date, she decided to take his breath away, and, peeling off her clothes, reached for a new set of undies, pure silk and costing a fortune, even though she had managed to get them wholesale—one of the perks of being a model. But she was a great believer in looking as good on the inside as the outside, convinced it helped boost the morale. Then she ran her eyes expertly over the dresses in her wardrobe, regretting she had only brought a small number with her. But at least she had had the sense to bring one eye-catcher, and she slipped into it and zipped it up. It was in red, a colour she rarely wore in summer. But it was as defiant as her mood, and anyway, come the winter, she would be guarding someone else, and Rees would be dating heaven knew who.

Her patent shoes and bag were black and shiny as her hair, which tonight she wore loose and curly, having given it a quick tong. It was very much an innocent pre-Raphaelite look, which contrasted wickedly with the daring cleavage of her dress which plunged almost to her waist, though the material was so skilfully cut that it gave only a tantalising glimpse of her full breasts.

When she swayed into the living-room, Rees's silence spoke volumes. But his hand on her elbow as he guided her into the elevator was unusually solicitous, as though she was something fragile that might break, and he ushered her into his car in the same manner.

He was looking pretty delectable himself, his perfectly cut dinner-jacket enhancing his lithe body, and making her aware of its latent strength. For a man who spent so many hours poring over a drawing-board, he was in excellent shape. But then, he got his exercise bouncing up and down on a bed!

They reached the Ritz and, leaving his car to be parked by a porter, they entered the hotel.

It was not one Julia knew well, and she was enchanted by the restaurant, with its rococo décor and the wide windows that opened on to a flower-filled terrace. It was a room designed to make the best of a woman, the lights muted and rosy, the furnishings pastel.

They were shown to a table by the window, but Julia, ever mindful of Rees' safety, and conscious of the many vantage points on the terrace where an assassin could hide, shook her head and pointed to one in the corner of the room.

'But this is the best table, madam,' the waiter said, shocked that she should decline it.

'I have hayfever, and the flowers on the terrace will make me sneeze,' she lied.

Instantly they were shown to the table of her choice, though Rees' faintly suspicious regard showed he had not swallowed the reason she had given.

'My apartment's full of flowers,' he murmured, 'and you haven't sneezed once.'

'This table is much more romantic,' she invented. 'We're not overlooked and—you can put your hand on my knee without anyone watching.'

He did it too, his fingers warm on the top of her thigh, and she jerked back, colour flaming into her face.

'Sorry, darling,' he drawled, 'but you did suggest it, and I got carried away.'

'That's exactly what you'll be, if you try it again,' she asserted, and he grinned mischievously.

'So tell me the real reason you want to sit here.'

'Because it's safer for you. I haven't forgotten that man's telephone call, even if *you* have.'

The sudden stillness of his body told her she had surprised him, but, being Rees and determined to play the macho man, he ignored her answer and beckoned the waiter for the menu and the wine-list.

'I don't see you as a Ritz type,' she said when, their order given, they sat sipping champagne. 'I picture you at nightclubs and discos and smart restaurants.'

'The Ritz is a very smart restaurant,' he countered, the side of his mouth quirking with amusement.

'I know, but it's more——' She searched for the right word. 'More decorous.'

His laugh rang out, drawing several eyes to him, the male ones appraising, the women's lingering. 'I'm sorry you see me as such a rake, Julia,' he said when he could speak, 'but that's only because you're so naïve.'

'Sorry,' she said, tossing back her champagne. 'I'll try not to bore you to death.'

'You'll never do that.' He paused, head to one side, almost as if he were mulling over what he had said, which he was, as his next words proved. 'To be honest, you're the least boring female I know. But I'm damned if I can figure out why.'

It was the first compliment he had paid her that she thoroughly liked. Used to being told she was beautiful, sexy, alluring, she couldn't ever remember being paid this particular compliment, and wondered if Rees knew what a lovely one it was.

'Do your other girlfriends bore you, then?' she asked carefully.

'I never thought so until now, but comparing them with you, I suppose the answer is yes. You seem to be three different people, so I never know where I am with you, and which one I'm going to encounter: the efficient PA, the little homebody—even though she can't cook—or the enchanting, sexy girl I'm out with tonight.'

'Let's see if I can guess which one you prefer,' she said sarcastically.

'You might be wrong.' His eyes ranged over her, but his expression was enigmatic. 'They say variety is the spice of life, and you're such a variety of people that I think it must be part of your charm.' He raised his glass. 'Let's drink to that, shall we? To the three faces of Julia. Each one more intriguing than the next.'

Pleasure coursed through her. It was rather like coming in from the cold and finding oneself in a room with a log fire. It was a fanciful simile, but she could think of none that more aptly described her feelings. Rees was a charmer all right, and she would do well to remember that charmers also knew how to keep their emotions intact.

But what do I care if it isn't lasting? she thought. It's nice at the time, so I might as well enjoy it.

Yet she could not quite give herself over to the mood, for she was constantly on the alert for Rees' safety. Still, they had their back to the wall so he could only be attacked from the front. Her eyes scanned the nearby diners, but they all looked innocent enough. Well-groomed, well-heeled men and women happily enjoying themselves. Yet she dared not lower her guard for a second, for even in the most unlikely places danger could threaten.

But the evening was uneventful from a security point of view, though emotionally she found it disquieting. She was liking Rees more and more, and wished she could truly be herself with him. Yet, if she were, he'd swiftly set about seducing her, which would bring her back to square one!

It was not until they were sipping their coffee that Rees surprised her by asking her about her background, and she decided to be as truthful as she could, without disclosing the real nature of her current job.

'I was born and brought up in the country,' she said casually. 'My father's ex-army turned farmer, and I have four brothers. When I was a child there was lots of laughter and teasing, trees to climb, rivers to fish and swim in, and the usual things one does in the country.'

'Sounds delightful.'

'It was—is. I miss it terribly.'

Rees leaned forward. 'So what brought you to this wicked city?'

'An urge to spread my wings.'

'And now you've spread them?'

'I'll fly a little longer. But one day I'll head for home. What about you?' she asked.

'A country upbringing like yours, though there the similarity ends. I have no siblings, and when I was nine my mother went off to Monaco with her tax exile lover. My father was killed in a car accident shortly afterwards.' He paused a moment before continuing, 'I never believed it was an accident as the coroner said. My father was a first-rate driver and knew the road too well to overshoot the bend.'

'You think he . . .' Julia's voice trailed away and Rees nodded.

'I think he didn't want to go on living after my mother left. He had loved her since they were in kindergarten together, and couldn't contemplate life without her.'

Julia was shocked. 'But he had you. Surely for your sake...'

'I wasn't compensation enough.'

Another question hovered, and Julia had to ask it. 'What happened then? Did you live with your mother?'

'She was too busy. By that time she had left her lover and opened an art gallery in New York. She flew over to see me once at school and charmed all the boys, even though she was wearing the most ridiculous hat.'

Julia could picture the scene all too well. The shy schoolboy, deeply missing his mother who, looking like an exotic bird, had suddenly presented herself to him. 'You loved her, didn't you?' she said softly.

'I suppose I must have done.' Rees' eyes were hooded, his face a mask she could not read. 'She's still running a gallery, but in Boca Rotan—a resort for the rich in Florida,' he explained.

The very lack of emotion in his voice spoke of a much deeper emotion that he would not release, that he might not even be aware of, and Julia's heart ached for the nine-year-old boy who had to come to terms with the knowledge that his mother had put her lover before him, and that, even when he was left fatherless, she had made no move to accept her responsibility.

'Where did you live after your father died?'

'I spent my vacations with my paternal aunt and uncle.'

He vouchsafed no more, and Julia did not press him. But what he had said had painted a bleak picture that explained why he was the cynical man of today, who was never going to become dependent on a woman.

'Don't go all dewy-eyed on me.'

Rees' voice, resonant and curt, broke the silence and shattered her mood. But it did not shatter the conclusions she had come to about him. Ruefully she acknowledged she had stepped away from the platonic relationship which Murray considered essential between a Guardian and the person they were protecting, and had now become emotionally as well as professionally caring of Rees's safety.

Too caring, she thought soberly, knowing that, for her own peace of mind, the sooner this assignment was over the better.

CHAPTER EIGHT

'JULIA, is that you?'

'Chris!' She nearly dropped the receiver in surprise. 'How did you know where to find me?'

'Your mother told me you were working for Engineering 2000 and I thought she was having me on. Last time we met you were singing the praises of Guardians.'

'Well... a woman's prerogative and all that.' Hastily she launched into the explanation she had given everyone other than her parents, that security was far duller than she had expected, and also too demanding.

'If that means you aren't so tied up,' Chris said at once, 'I'm glad to hear it. I'm off to New Zealand and I'd like to see you before I go.'

'A new job?' she asked.

'Yes. I think I've hit the jackpot this time.'

She hoped he had. But then, from what she could gather, he was always hitting the jackpot, then coming a cropper. She didn't even bother asking what the jackpot was.

'So when can I see you?' he asked.

'I'm afraid I'm tied up,' she lied. 'We've a sales conference on all week, and I rarely finish before midnight.'

That should put paid to Chris, she decided, paling at the thought of him bringing her back to the penthouse and bumping into Rees. Sure as chickens laid eggs, he'd blurt out she'd been in security work, and it wouldn't take Rees long to guess that she still was, and send her packing. Not that she would be sorry to leave, for, the sooner she was out of his orbit, the better for her peace of mind. Yet what peace would she have if her departure left him open to an assassin's bullet? If only the police soon discovered something concrete. But they were still no nearer finding out who had made the threats against Rees' life, and Julia was coming to the conclusion that only when the man—or woman—made their move against him would they know. She had learned from Murray only yesterday that Rees would soon be signing the all-important American contract, and once he did he would be out on the town again and leaving himself wide open to be struck down.

Already his girlfriends were ringing to find out why they had not heard from him, and she had occasionally gone into his office and heard him sweet-talking them. How furious it made her to see him perusing a document or signing his letters at the same time, his mind clearly not on any of the sweet nothings he was mouthing. And 'sweet nothings' was a very apt description, for nothing was what he felt for Dawn and Clarissa and the countless others whose names she didn't know!

'Daydreaming?' Rees' deep voice made her aware he had come into the office. His cheeks were flushed, and his eyes, always bright, had an extra gleam in their dark brown depths.

'Good news?' she asked, aware he had come from a meeting with Sir Andrew.

'Yes. I'm finalising something tomorrow, and I'll be free to——' He stopped abruptly, as if once again remembering Julia knew nothing about his business deals, nor why he had led such an exemplary life these past few weeks.

'You mean the American contract with that religious Mr Bargett?' she queried, hiding a smile as she saw Rees grow rigid.

'Who told you about it?'

'I have my sources.'

'Who?'

'I also know it's the only reason you let me move in with you,' she parried, striving to look wide-eyed. 'Because you were scared I'd tell everyone you'd played fast and loose with me, and Mr Bargett might hear of it.'

'I most certainly didn't play fast and loose with you!' he grated. 'You childishly assumed that because I wanted to make love to you I wanted to marry you. Dammit, Julia, it's time you grew up!' Upon which remark, he strode into his office and slammed the door.

Julia felt a spark of sympathy for him. No girl in today's world would be as naïve as the character she was portraying, and it had been kind-hearted of him to believe her sob story about having nowhere to live and letting her move in with him. But what was she thinking? He hadn't done it out of kindness, but in order to protect his good name.

But once the deal was concluded he would have no more worries, and she was sure that within the next few days he would tell her to go. Julia's eyebrows knit together in a frown. There had to be a way of stopping him, though for the moment nothing came to mind.

With a sigh she reached for his diary to check on his next appointment. As she did, an idea came to mind and her eyes lit with satisfaction. If Rees asked her to leave his apartment, she would threaten to walk out on her job. This would mean his having to hire someone else, not something a busy man would relish doing, especially when he knew Mrs Williamson would soon be returning. Yes, that was her solution.

For the rest of the afternoon she saw nothing of Rees, who spent several hours with one of the senior engineers in the workshop-cum-laboratory that took up the entire basement floor.

It was five-thirty before he returned to his office, his hair dishevelled, his collar loosened, with the look of pleasure on his face he always wore when he had been 'messing about' with machinery.

How like little boys men were, she thought, feeling an upsurge of affection for him, and resisting the urge to lean forward and wipe off the smut of oil marking the firm chin.

'Sir Andrew would like to see you,' she said.

With barely a glance in her direction, he strode out again, leaving Julia to tidy her desk and wonder how long it would be before they went home.

At six-thirty she was still wondering, and when her watch showed seven, she was convinced he had gone home without telling her. Surely he wouldn't be so mean? Yet why not? He was furious with her and this would be a good way of showing it. As the thought crossed her mind, the door opened to admit him.

'Sorry I'm late, Julia.'

She shrugged and reached for her jacket, a navy silk blazer that complemented her navy pleated skirt and sleeveless, silky white top.

'I like your idea of a business outfit,' he commented drily.

'Navy and white is very serviceable.' Her voice was prim. 'And the blouse is high-necked.'

'So it is.' He eyed her. 'I guess you'd look sexy even in a sack.'

Her heart thumped as if he had given her the most wonderful compliment, but she said nothing and demurely did up the gilt buttons.

'I thought we'd eat out tonight,' he went on.

'But Mrs Hartley's prepared——'

'We'll eat it tomorrow. I'm fed up staying at home.'

Julia's spirits lifted, realising that for these two days at least he wasn't turfing her out. 'I'd just as soon stay home,' she said. 'There's a good programme on television and——'

'We're eating out.'

Accepting the order, she followed him down to the car park, hoping he wouldn't choose a restaurant that left him open to attack.

In the event, they went to another French bistro, a stone's throw from his apartment, and entering the small room—it held no more than a dozen tables—her apprehension lessened, for she'd have no difficulty monitoring everyone who came in.

To her surprise the owner, a plump, voluble man, greeted Rees like a long-lost friend, and the two men indulged in a long conversation in French which she only just managed to follow. Watching Rees' face light up as he heard the latest exploits of Philippe's youngest son, increased her conviction that he had turned away from love because of his mother and his determination not to be hurt again, and she found herself hoping he would meet a girl who'd touch his heart. There were so many fine things about him, so many springs untapped, that it would be a waste if he lived his life on the surface, eschewing love and commitment lest it lead to pain.

With a start she realised Rees was speaking to her. 'Sorry,' she apologised, 'I was miles away.'

'With whom?'

'No one. To be honest, I was thinking of *you*.'

'Not very pleasant thoughts, by the look on your face!'

'I was actually hoping that one day you'll fall in love.'

'What a morbid wish. You'd better have a drink to cheer you up!'

'Fruit juice for me, please.'

'On the wagon again?'

She did not answer, and concentrated on the menu.

During the meal they chatted idly on a host of subjects, making Julia realise they were never short of things to say to each other. Funny what an easy man Rees was to talk to, when he gave the impression of being aloof and uninterested in other people's opinions. More than any man she knew, his façade belied the inner person, and she was cogitating on this when he almost echoed her thoughts.

'You're a strange girl, Julia—one moment childish, the next perceptive and profound.'

'You keep saying that,' she reminded him.

'And I keep wondering which is the real you.'

'Guess.'

'I wouldn't waste my time. Women can change their moods and beliefs to suit themselves.'

She understood his cynicism, but none the less deplored it. 'You see us as very expedient, don't you?'

'That shouldn't surprise you.'

'Well, it does. It's childish to judge all women on the basis of one.'

'I'm acquainted with quite a few,' he said curtly, 'and I can't say any have struck me as being anything other than vain and self-centred.'

'*All* the women you've met?' Julia countered, and was intrigued when his eyes looked away from hers and he visibly hesitated.

'Almost,' he said slowly.

'What happened to her?' Julia asked.

'Who?'

'The woman who was different.'

'She went back to Australia where she came from.'

'Were you in love with her?'

'Who said anything about love?' he retorted. 'I fancied her like mad and—and then I stopped fancying her.' He sipped his wine. 'Why do you always have to talk about my girlfriends? It seems to be your favourite topic of conversation.'

'Because I think it's your favourite occupation!'

'Well, you're wrong. My work comes first with me. In fact, it's my life.'

'How empty.'

'How rewarding,' he countered.

'I'll remind you of that in five years' time, when I have you to dinner in my happy home with my loving husband and adorable children!'

His teeth flashed in a grin. 'How happy I'll be to leave you and return to the peace of my own home, where I can eat what I like when I like, have total control of the television and stereo, with no one to tell me what to do and when to do it!'

The more he said, the more she realised how determined he was to remain a bachelor, a thought which inexplicably depressed her. But only because it seemed a waste of a gorgeous-looking man who had so much to offer. Though not to me, she told herself. We'd fight like cat and dog! I'm too determined and he's too obstinate. Or was it the other way round? But no matter. Either way they were incompatible.

She was aware of him watching her, and, strangely reluctant to meet his gaze, let her eyes roam the room. All the tables were full now, with diners who looked like regulars: couples and families who had come to their 'local' for what they knew would be a reliably good meal.

Her gaze stopped at a table by the door. By the door! An excellent spot for someone wanting to make a quick getaway. She craned to see who was sitting there, waiting impatiently for a waiter to move away. As he did, she saw a gaunt, grey-faced man in his mid-forties. But what alerted her was his menacing stare as he focused on each table, as though looking for someone. Now he was staring at their table, his head coming forward as if for a better view.

Rees turned at that moment to attract the attention of the waiter, and Julia saw the man by the door stealthily put his hand into the pocket of his jacket.

He was reaching for a gun! In one bound she jumped up and flung herself against Rees, knocking his wine-glass from his hand.

'Quick!' she cried. 'Under the table!'

'What?'

'Under the table!'

Shielding Rees with her body, she tried to pull him off his chair. Furiously he resisted her, much to the amusement of the other diners, who assumed she had been overcome by lust. But Julia was beyond caring what anyone thought, intent only on saving Rees' life.

'Get under the table!' she shouted, clutching him round the neck. 'The man by the door—he's got a gun!'

'For God's sake, woman!' Rees bellowed, pushing her away from him and back into her chair. 'That's François, and he wouldn't hurt a fly.'

Julia's mouth fell open. 'François? You know him?'

'Everyone who comes here does. He sits at that table every night, planning how to get even with his wife who ran off with his best friend.' Rees turned round and waved a greeting to the man by the door before turning back to Julia, his eyes brimming with amusement. 'Did you think he was a killer?'

'You've got to admit he looks like one, and he kept staring our way.'

'He probably fancies you!'

'Must you bring everything down to sex?' she said crossly.

'Can you think of anything better?'

Irritably she looked away, still aware of the chuckles around her. What an idiot she must seem. Still, as Murray would say, better safe than sorry. And if François *had* been the assassin . . .

It was still early when they returned home, and though Julia instantly retired to her room she was too restless and edgy to sleep. After showering and slipping on a housecoat that covered her from top to toe—she was taking no chances with Rees—she wandered into the living-room and found him immersed in papers.

Settling into the corner of a couch, she wondered if switching on the television would disturb him.

'It won't bother me,' he said, as if divining her thoughts, and indicated the remote control pad lying on the table in front of him.

Keeping the volume low, Julia watched the news. She found it difficult to concentrate, too aware of Rees beside her, jacket and tie off, shirt unbuttoned to show a tanned chest.

He was completely oblivious of her presence as he studied the papers on his lap, occasionally pursing his mouth—what a well-shaped mouth it was for a man—and frequently scribbling in the margin, his gold pen glinting against long, lean fingers.

There was not one physical thing about him she would change, she decided, musing how unfair it was of nature to give a man so much and not also give him a desire for marriage!

'I want to thank you, Julia.'

His voice startled her out of her absorption. 'Thank me for what?'

'Offering me your body.' There was humour in his voice, though his eyes remained serious.

'I did no such thing,' she said indignantly.

'Yes, you did—in the restaurant. If François had been out to kill me, the bullet would have hit you in the middle of your delectable back.'

Only then did she realise that, in her desire to protect Rees, she had given no thought to her own safety. But that was what she had been trained for, wasn't it? No, the answer came back. She had been trained to protect her client, but not to put her own life directly in the firing line.

'Of course, accidents will happen, and you may get hurt,' Murray had said during one of their training sessions. 'But your main job at all times is to be watchful and prevent a dangerous situation from arising, not to put yourselves at risk.'

But, as Rees had so rightly said, she had done exactly that, and knew that if necessary she would do it again, for she loved this man. Loved him with all her heart, and could not envisage life without him.

My God! What had she said? Stunned, she was powerless to think. All she experienced were overwhelming feelings whose intensity scared her: feelings of tenderness, passion, admiration, even anger at Rees' blindness in refusing to see so many things that were crystal clear to her.

How blind I was not to know, she thought soberly. But now that I do, what *am* I going to do? At the moment there was only one answer to this question. She would stay with Rees and protect him.

'Nothing to say for yourself?' he murmured into the silence. 'Or do you always go around trying to save your escort's life?'

'When they're as obstinate as *you*, yes!'

Rees dumped his papers on to the table and came to sit on the settee beside her. 'Even though I think you're worrying about me for nothing, I was touched by what you did, especially since you still see me as a seducer out to get my way with you.'

'Not any more I don't,' she said quickly, afraid that if he made a pass at her she wouldn't be able to hide her feelings for him. 'You've—you've behaved in an exemplary manner since I moved in with you. Just like a brother.'

'I don't feel like your brother. I feel I want to be your lover!' Lifting her hair with a gentle hand, he lightly pressed a kiss on the nape of her neck.

His touch sent tremors through her, and he was instantly aware of it and pulled her swiftly into his arms, at the same time pressing her down on to the cushions.

Julia knew she should resist him, but the touch of his hands—like fire on her body—burned away her resolve, and she made no demur as he skilfully unbuttoned her housecoat and buried his face in the softness of her breasts, suckling first one nipple, then the other, till they rose in hard, throbbing points. Only then did his mouth leave them to feather little kisses up her neck, and then higher still to part her lips with his questing tongue, and enter the soft, inner moistness.

With wild abandon she drank him in, breathing in the scent of him, exulting in the feel of his body, the weight of his limbs and the stirring between his thighs. Desire rushed through her like a river in flood, scattering her senses, and she gripped him tightly, thrilling to his muffled groan as his hands slowly explored her, cupping the fullness of her breasts, curving around her hips to grasp her buttocks and raise them till her soft curves pressed tightly against his hard stomach and the throbbing swell of his arousal.

It aroused an answering need in her that couldn't be denied, and she parted her legs and twined them around his hips, uncaring that she was leaving herself open to him, knowing only that she wanted him inside her, filling her with his life force.

'You're beautiful,' he gasped. 'So beautiful, I want to kiss every inch of you... every inch.'

He began to do so, leaving a moist trail down the velvety skin of her thighs and the softer skin where curly dark hair shielded the pulsing bud that no man had ever touched. But she wanted Rees to, wanted to give herself entirely to him, abandon herself to his hands, his mouth, his tongue that was even now penetrating the dark mysterious depths of her virginity. Never had she felt such overpowering desire, such deep longing, and she threshed wildly and arched her body to his.

'Yes, yes,' he cried. 'Let me love you; let me take you.'

Dimly the words penetrated her mind. 'Let me love you, let me take you.' But not 'I love you'. She was only a body to him, a receptacle for his passion; nothing more. She shivered with the pain of it, the knowledge robbing her of all passion and leaving her cold as the grave. What a fitting word, she thought bleakly. The grave of all her hopes...

'No, Rees!' she whispered, and tried to push him away. 'I can't.'

'You can. We want each other,' he muttered deep in his throat and sought her mouth again, his tongue wild within her, penetrating so deeply that it was like the sexual act itself.

She tried to turn her head, but was powerless to move, and instead she made an effort to control the response of her body. But, oh God, how difficult it was when his fingers were playing her as though she were a violin, finding the crevices, the curves, the beating pulse that ached for him.

'Let me enter you,' he gasped. 'Julia, *darling*...'

'No!' she cried. *'Not without love.'*

Her words fell like ice-shards between them, shattering the passion that had almost made them one, and they were two people again, with an ever-widening gulf between them, a gulf that had always been there, though for a brief moment she had almost believed he had crossed it.

'Still clinging to your romantic illusions?' he asked with irony, his words showing how firmly he was entrenched on the far side.

'Yes,' she said, gathering her housecoat around her, and with it her pride. 'I'll never change my mind, Rees. Sex without love is meaningless.'

'Sex without love can be exhilarating, exciting and a wonderful release of emotion and tension.'

'I prefer a hot bath.' She stood up and, though it required an effort, looked him full in the face. 'I'm sure sex without love can be everything you say it is, but *with* love it can give your life a whole new dimension.'

'I'm happy as I am,' he shrugged, and turned away from her.

Heartbroken, she stared at his broad-shouldered back, noticing the proud way he held his head. She waited for him to ask her to move out of his home, and wondered what problems this would create for Murray Guardian and herself. Her mind raced madly, only stopping as Rees spoke.

'You won't need to lock your bedroom door, Julia.'

'I'm delighted to hear it,' she retorted. 'Even *my* love can't last if it isn't nourished, and I've gone off you in a very big way.'

'Then there's no harm done,' he said, returning to his chair and papers.

'Except to your pride.'

'It would take more than a turn-down from *you* to dent that.'

Giving him the last word, she marched from the room. Her bravado lasted only till she was alone, and she sank down on her bed and stared into a future that was going to be very bleak without him. Yet better bleakness than the pain and bitterness she would feel if she compromised her beliefs. Blinking back the tears, she stood up and went to the window.

It was a beautiful clear night, with a full moon in the sky sending a pattern of light across the terrace. Since moving in here she had made sure the terrace lights were kept on till daybreak, pretending she liked to look out of her bedroom window and see the flowers in their decorative urns, when in reality it was to ensure that any trespasser could be seen.

Unlocking the glass door, she walked outside. Though midnight, the air was still warm, and she wandered across to the edge of the patio and looked down at the Thames, dark and gleaming. In a week's time, or a month—surely it would not be longer?—she would be gone from Rees' life, with Mrs Williamson taking over from her in the office, and some blonde, brunette or redhead making her a fading memory in Rees' mind. But it would be a long while before he was out of her own, and for the briefest of moments she was tempted to go to him and let him make love to her, so she would at least have some happy memories as consolation.

Yet, aware that what they shared would only be sex, those memories wouldn't satisfy her for long, and sombrely she left the terrace and went to bed; alone, unhappy, yet strangely content in the knowledge that she had done the right thing.

CHAPTER NINE

NEXT day Rees behaved as though nothing had happened between them. Of course, nothing *had*, Julia reminded herself, piqued that he had so quickly written her off. But then, as he had made abundantly clear, he wasn't going to waste his time trying to seduce the unseduceable!

Telling herself it was for the best, she determinedly matched his mood, and anyone coming into the office and seeing them together would never have guessed that the previous night they had been lying in a passionate embrace, skin upon skin, devouring mouth upon throbbing breasts.

Whether it was on purpose or by intent, Rees was kept inordinately busy that day, going from one meeting to another, and taking Julia with him to nearly all of them to make notes. He appeared to have forgotten she did not do shorthand, and she was hard put to it to get all the salient points down. But luckily she had a retentive memory, and in the apartment later that evening she began adding to the notes she had made. By the time she had finished, her hand was aching, and she flung her pen down with relief. Another day like today and she would take one of the secretaries along with her.

She was still gently massaging her wrist when the telephone rang, and a lilting, feminine voice asked to speak to Rees. But this one had an Australian accent, and Julia, who tried to monitor all his calls, had never spoken to her before.

'You don't sound like Mrs Hartley,' the girl said. 'Are you the new housekeeper or a girlfriend?'

'Neither,' Julia said crisply. 'I'm Rees' assistant, and I *do* mean assistant.'

A warm laugh came across the line. 'I'm Melinda Harrison, and I'd like to speak to Rees.'

'He's in the shower. But I'll tell him as soon as he comes out. Does he have your number?'

'Yes. Tell him I've managed to rent the same apartment—just around the corner from him.'

Julia was replacing the receiver when Rees came in, clad in a towelling robe.

'One of your girlfriends just called,' she said. 'Melinda Harrison.'

'What?' Rees looked stunned, then his mobile mouth widened into a smile of pure delight. 'Melinda *here*? In England?'

Only then did Julia recollect Rees telling her that he had fancied one girl above all others and that she had returned to Australia when he had stopped fancying her. But the happiness now on his face belied his words, and Julia was filled with fury, anguish and misery, all of which she belatedly recognised as nothing more than jealousy. Oh, God, she thought, what is this man doing to me? I've always hated jealousy. It's a demeaning emotion and shows a lack of self-esteem. Yet jealousy was what she felt, and there was nothing she could do to stop it as Rees reached for the telephone.

'Did she say where she's staying?'

'She's in her old apartment.'

Swiftly he dialled. No problem about him forgetting the number, Julia thought miserably. It must be engraved on his heart. Hurriedly she gathered her notes together, but Rees was already talking.

'It's wonderful to hear your voice! Why didn't you let me know? Of course I'm free. I'll be with you as soon as I've changed.' His head tilted to one side as he listened, his full lower lip curving into a smile. 'Sure you can,' he said. 'Come over and have a drink with her. Then I'll take you to Annabel's for dinner.'

'Melinda wants to see you for yourself,' he said, putting down the receiver and grinning at Julia. 'She says, knowing my reputation, she doesn't believe you're only my assistant!'

'Shall I take off my make-up and dig out a pair of glasses?'

'Even a false nose wouldn't make you ugly! Just act naturally and let Melinda judge for herself. She's no fool.'

'You amaze me,' Julia retorted. 'Only a fool could go on fancying you!'

Rees laughed. 'Good thing you have a sense a humour. It's one of your better qualities.'

She warned herself to watch her tongue. There was too much at stake—Rees' life—to put a foot wrong.

Tossing her head, she walked out, but, once in her room, paced the floor anxiously. There was no way of preventing Rees from going out with Melinda, and no way of getting herself invited. She could imagine his face if she suggested it! Yet she dared not leave him unguarded, and in desperation she telephoned Murray.

'I don't have anyone free,' he informed her when she told him the problem.

'But *someone* has to watch him.'

'Too right. Will *I* do?'

'Of course you'll do,' she exclaimed. 'But I didn't think you worked in the field any more.'

'Only when there's an emergency. And tonight there is. Shall I pick you up, or will you cadge a lift with Rees and his lady-love?'

Julia was flummoxed. 'Cadge a lift where?'

'To Annabel's, where else? If I'm playing protector for a night, I intend it to be with a beautiful girl in tow. So get your glad rags on, sweetheart. We're dining and dancing together.'

Julia's eyes sparkled at the thought of Rees' face when he saw her at the nightclub with a good-looking man like Murray. Oh, boy, his nose would really be out of joint! Except why should it, when his nose was pointed firmly in Melinda's direction?

'You still there?' Murray asked.

'I was just thinking. Call me back in ten minutes and ask me for a date. That will make it look authentic, because Rees and I were supposed to be staying in tonight.'

With Murray promising to do as she asked, Julia took out the dress she had bought during her lunch break today, a flowery chiffon in pink and violet. It had practically beckoned at her from the window of a boutique, and because she had been filled with miserable thoughts over Rees she had extravagantly treated herself to it. But she dared not put it on yet, not until Murray had called and Rees had overheard the conversation. Picking up a book, she went back to the living-room.

She was half-way down the hall when the doorbell rang and Rees dashed from his room, pulled the door open and a smiling girl into his arms.

Hurriedly Julia turned away, but Rees called her.

'Hey, Julia, come and meet Melinda.'

Summoning a smile, she took the girl's outstretched hand. Prepared to dislike her, Julia instantly felt a rapport. Not only was Melinda stunningly pretty, tall and slender, with hair the colour of corn, but she also had a genuine smile, and a humorous gleam in her big brown eyes.

'Are you really his assistant?' Melinda asked, her voice even more melodious than on the telephone. 'Or is Rees too diplomatic to tell me you're his latest?'

'I've never considered him diplomatic,' Julia said, 'and I'm definitely not his latest.'

'Even though she's living here,' Rees put in smoothly, and Julia, watching the Australian girl, saw the statement had come as a shock.

'I was turned out of my apartment and haven't yet managed to find anything else,' she explained quickly, determined not to let Rees think she wanted to make mischief between him and his lady-love. 'In fact I turned up on Rees's doorstep with my cases and bludgeoned him into taking me in.'

'Chalk that up as a victory,' Melinda said. 'I've never known Rees be bludgeoned into doing anything he didn't want to do.'

'When you two have finished dissecting me...' Firmly pushing them both into the living-room, he went to the bar. 'What will you have, Melinda?'

'The usual,' she smiled, and there was a world of intimacy in the two words as well as in the look that passed between them.

'And you, Julia?'

It was a wonder he had remembered she was there, Julia thought sourly. 'I'll have the usual, too,' she replied, but there was no intimacy in *her* words, and definitely none in the way Rees didn't look at her when he handed her an orange juice and then turned to uncork a bottle of champagne.

Melinda accepted a glass from him and waited while he poured his own.

Julia, anticipating an intimate toast, was even more jealous when Rees simply touched his goblet to Melinda's mouth before drinking from it. Then he caught her hand and drew her down on to the couch beside him.

Julia knew that the decent thing was to leave them alone, but deciding that since Rees had given her an orange juice he did not expect her to sip it in solitary state, she perched on a chair a little distance away from them.

'How come you're back in London?' Rees questioned the girl beside him.

'I'm doing some cosmetic commercials.' Melinda settled back comfortably and crossed one shapely leg over the other.

'How long will you be here?'

'As long as I like. My agent says he can get me masses of work.'

'That's great. At least, I hope it is?'

There was an electric silence between them, as tangible as if a spark had flashed, and then Melinda gave a faint sigh and commented, 'Doesn't my ringing you give you your answer?'

The dark head nodded, and Julia was unable to bear any more. She was half-way to the door when the telephone rang, and she slowed her step.

'Sure,' Rees said into the receiver. 'She's right here.' He held out the phone to her. 'For you.'

'For me?' she asked with pseudo-innocence, then allowed a look of pleasure to cross her face as she heard the voice at the other end.

'Mark, *darling*! I didn't realise you were back in town. Of course I'm free. I've been a real stay-at-home since you left London. I know, darling. I've missed you too.' Julia made herself pause while Murray chuckled at the other end, and then told her to get on with her act. 'I'd love to go to Annabel's,' she said. 'Hang on a moment.' She looked at Rees. 'Mark lives in Highgate, and if he has to come all the way down here to collect me——'

'We can give you a lift, can't we, Rees?' Melinda cut in.

'No problem,' he said. 'But you'll have to make your own way back.'

It was all Julia could do not to throw her drink at him. 'How unusual of you to state the obvious,' she said sweetly, then turned to make her arrangements with 'Mark'.

'If you ladies will excuse me, I'll go and finish dressing,' Rees said.

'Me, too,' Julia added. 'I'd no idea I was going out tonight.'

'Don't mind me,' Melinda smiled. 'I can do with a cat nap.' She curled up in a corner of the couch, showing more than a glimpse of creamy thigh, then closed her eyes.

Julia walked ahead of Rees down the corridor, very conscious of him behind her.

'I'm glad you've a date tonight,' he said. 'I wouldn't want you to stay at home alone and be bored.'

'That's sweet of you,' Julia said with false sincerity. 'Mark's an old flame of mine.'

'Not a very hot one, or you wouldn't be going out with him.'

'Mark respects me,' Julia said primly.

'He must be under-sexed!'

For answer, she closed the door in his face.

Curiosity to find out more about Melinda gave Julia the speed of lightning, and she was dressed and back in the living-room within ten minutes. Unfortunately Melinda had fallen asleep, her long hair a soft, golden cloud around her.

Julia flung her bag on to the floor, hoping to wake her. It did, and sleepy brown eyes blinked at her.

'I think jet lag's caught up with me.' Melinda yawned prettily. 'I flew in this morning.'

'And you called Rees straight away?' Julia tried to sound disinterested.

'I almost called him from Sydney before I left, but I didn't want to give him the chance to run!'

The girl swung her legs to the ground and lazily stretched. Her every movement was graceful, and Julia, no slouch herself when it came to looks, accepted that Melinda was a natural beauty in the Australian mould: tall, blonde and tanned, with a warmth and vivacity that girls in the southern hemisphere always seemed to have.

'How long have you worked for Rees?' Melinda asked. 'I never thought Mrs Williamson would ever leave him.'

Julia launched into her well-rehearsed explanation for the woman's temporary leave.

'Will you be sorry to go when she comes back?' Melinda enquired.

'No. I'm counting the days, actually.' She decided it was her turn to be inquisitor. 'Have you known Rees long?'

'Four years. But I haven't seen him for eighteen months. We quarrelled and I went back to Australia.'

The girl lapsed into silence, her lovely face sad, and, though Julia was as full of curiosity as a puppy, she didn't feel she had the right to pry further.

'We lived together for nearly two years,' Melinda went on softly, almost as if speaking to herself, 'and then I tried to push him into marriage by giving him an ultimatum. I lost, of course. He said he loved me, but that he'd never marry *anyone*, and I was so angry and upset, I walked out.'

'And you're back to do some commercials?'

'I'm back because I wanted to be. I've as much work in Australia as I can handle. But I needed an excuse to see Rees and find out if there's someone else in his life, or if I can move into it again.'

'Without marriage?' Julia kept her voice even.

'On any terms he'll have me. I nearly married someone else a few months ago, but then found I couldn't go through with it. So here I am.'

Julia was sincerely sorry for Melinda. She obviously cared for Rees, while he, in his inimitable fashion, cared only for himself. But wasn't she judging him too harshly? After all, he made no secret of his determination to stay single, and if Melinda finally accepted this they'd probably be very happy.

'*Is* there anyone else in his life?' Melinda asked.

Julia was tempted to lie, then honesty won the day and she shook her head. 'He's still playing the field, from what I gather.'

Melinda seemed decidedly happier, though Julia's mood swung in the opposite direction. If only I didn't like the girl, she thought, but she's so warm and friendly, it's easy to see why Rees still cares for her. No way could she see him turning down the chance of having Melinda back. If the girl played her cards more carefully this time, she might eventually even lead him into marriage.

'I won't make the mistake of pushing him this time,' Melinda said, as if echoing Julia's thoughts. 'Rees never looked at another girl the two years he was with me, and if I can settle for that...' She gave the faintest of smiles. 'Perhaps if we have a child later on, he might change his mind.'

Julia's spirits plummeted to an all-time low, and though she tried to look uncaring the keen look Melinda gave her told her she had not succeeded. For a moment she was tempted to admit she was also in love with Rees, then knew nothing would be served by doing so. Before the night was out, Melinda would be in his bed and she herself a fading memory.

'Ready?' Rees asked from the door, and Melinda went across to him. Julia was filled with despair. They looked so right for each other. He tall, dark and handsome, she blonde and willowy. Feeling like a third wheel, Julia went down with them to the foyer.

'I intend drinking a magnum of champagne to celebrate your return,' he said, shepherding Melinda into a taxi, and then doing so more perfunctorily for Julia. 'So it's best if I don't drive.'

Julia, ever conscious that she was guarding Rees' life, was glad he was saved the necessity of parking and could go straight from the cab into the shelter of Annabel's. With this in mind, she jumped out of the taxi almost before it had halted outside the club, and with the open door of the cab protecting Rees on one side, she was careful to make sure she shielded him on the other.

Murray had not yet arrived, but he had rung to say he was delayed, and she was shown to the table he had booked, which luckily was not too far from Rees'. Flailing herself, Julia watched him devote his attention to Melinda, sitting close beside her on the banquette and smiling into her eyes. So intently was she watching him that she didn't notice Murray until she felt his hand on her arm, and she looked up, startled.

She was even more startled when she took in his appearance, for she had never before seen him dressed for an evening out. In the office he generally wore navy trousers and sweater, and the few occasions he had supervised her training course, he had worn denims. But tonight he was resplendent in a grey silk mohair suit, his wavy golden hair brushed sleek. A pale blue shirt drew attention to his tanned skin, and made his eyes appear an even deeper blue.

'You look gorgeous,' he said, sliding on to the banquette beside her.

'So do you.'

He appraised her frankly, as if enjoying the sight of her heart-shaped face framed by her lustrous black hair; her slender, yet curvaceous body enticingly covered in soft chiffon. 'You look good enough to eat.'

'Hey,' she said. 'This is a business date, remember? It's not supposed to be for real.'

'Sorry. I guess the sight of you carried me away.'

Teasingly, she flexed her muscles. 'Make sure I don't get you carried away permanently!'

He laughed. 'OK, so let's stick to business. Where's Denton?'

'Three tables to the right, sitting with a gorgeous blonde.'

Murray dropped his napkin to the floor and, bending to pick it up, used the opportunity to check out exactly where Rees was. 'Shall we order and then dance?' Then, before she had a chance to reply, Murray jumped up and pulled her to her feet. 'Sorry, but Denton's dancing and so must we.'

Though tall and broad, Murray was light on his feet, and, without appearing to, adroitly kept on Rees' heels.

Julia tried not to see Rees dancing cheek to cheek with Melinda, and resisted the urge to close her eyes, remembering that she and Murray had to keep them wide open in this ever-moving, ever-changing throng.

The music seemed to go on for ever—slow, smoochy music, when she longed for something bright and brash, for anything to keep Melinda from nestling close in Rees' arms.

'I like the scent you're wearing,' Murray murmured.

'I forgot to put any on,' Julia confessed.

'You mean the lovely smell is you?'

'Stop flirting with me, Murray.'

'I'm doing it to make Denton jealous,' he protested. 'You've still got to stick close to him, you know.'

'Fat chance I'll have with Melinda back.'

'You can always blow your cover and tell him who you are.'

'He'd kick me out. He's the most stupidly obstinate man.'

'Obstinate or not, I think Sir Andrew's reached the stage where he'll give him an ultimatum if I say it's necessary.'

Julia debated whether this might not be the best course of action. With her subterfuge out of the way, she could do her job more easily and, in reverting to her proper role, might convince Rees that her feelings for him had merely been a hoax. Would that it were true! Watching the dark head bent to the fair one, she trembled with longing for him.

Feeling the movement, Murray drew her closer. 'Your feelings are showing.'

About to deny it, she changed her mind. Maybe if she told someone how she felt, she'd get it out of her system. After all, bearing in mind what she wanted from life, she was crazy to love a man like Rees.

'Stupid, aren't I?' she said.

'Denton's even more stupid for not seeing what's under his nose.'

'Oh, he saw,' Julia sighed, 'but he didn't want—except on a temporary basis.'

'You're lovely enough to make any man change his mind about that.'

'Not Rees, and certainly not now Melinda's back. She's the love of his life, you know.'

'You're going to find this job tough,' Murray muttered. 'Especially when they leave here. I hope his bedroom's sound-proofed.'

Julia's cheeks burned, and the images Murray's words evoked were so painful, it was a moment before she spoke. 'He'll probably go back to her place.'

'If he does, I'll take over from you and you can go home.'

'You don't need to wet-nurse me,' she said sharply. 'I'm perfectly capable of doing my job.'

'Too capable.'

'What does that mean?'

'That you've worn yourself to a frazzle guarding Denton. You've lost weight, and there are blue shadows under your eyes.'

'My weight fluctuates,' she lied. 'And the shadows are make-up. It's all the rage to look fragile this season.'

'Rubbish.' Murray gave her a little shake, then wrapped his arms around her again, at which moment Rees turned to lead Melinda off the floor, and saw them.

'Hello, Julia.' He looked directly at Murray, and she casually introduced them.

'Rees, this is Mark Gardner, an old friend of mine.'

'Not as old as all that,' Murray chuckled, and looked at Rees. 'I want to thank you for taking care of Julia when she had to leave that apartment she was in. But now I'm back, I'm going to see if I can make her move in with *me*.'

Julia was astonished and delighted by Murray's imagination, though her pleasure ebbed as Rees nodded and said equably, 'She's free to go any time.'

'Thanks for trying to make him jealous,' Julia murmured when they were out of Rees' earshot. 'But if you don't care about someone, you don't care what they do.'

'Well, nothing ventured, nothing gained. You're worth ten of that blonde.'

'Not true, boss. You're prejudiced.'

For the next couple of hours Julia did her best to act as if she were enjoying herself, though it was a relief when Murray glanced across her shoulder and said, 'I'll call for the bill. Rees and his lady-love are leaving.'

'He generally stays out later than this,' Julia commented before she could stop herself.

'When you've a beautiful and willing lady beside you, it can never be too soon to go home,' Murray chuckled.

'That's hardly a diplomatic comment to make to me,' Julia said brightly, deciding that, since Murray had guessed how she felt about Rees, it was better to wear her heart brazenly on her sleeve.

'I'm a great believer in the cold turkey treatment,' he replied. 'If you're convinced you don't stand a chance with him, you'll start looking for someone else.'

Murray's hand was warm around her waist as he escorted her from the room, and Julia suddenly wished she was his girl, and that Rees Denton meant nothing to her.

As they emerged from Annabel's, the object of her thoughts was being driven away in a cab, and she and Murray raced to his car, parked a few yards away.

'Do you know where Melinda's staying?' he asked, switching on the ignition. 'If we lose the cab, I want to know where to head for.'

'She has an apartment in Dockland Towers, round the corner from Rees.'

'We'll head there,' Murray said, setting the car in motion.

'And then?'

'I'll wait for him to come out, and you can go home and get your beauty sleep.'

Fat chance she had of sleeping, Julia thought miserably. All she'd do was pace the floor and think of Rees making love to Melinda, his mouth exploring hers, his supple fingers caressing her breasts, his strong legs entwined with paler, fragile ones. For the first time she wished she had never quit modelling, that she hadn't become a Guardian, and that she had never met Rees.

But she had, and her only chance of finding peace was to get him out of her system as fast as possible.

CHAPTER TEN

MURRAY drew his car quietly to a stop in the shadows—a few yards from the entrance to Docklands Towers—and switched off the engine. Julia had managed to get the number of Rees' cab as it had pulled away from Annabel's, and they had kept it in sight all the way. Murray was right, Julia thought as the cab drove off, empty, Rees *is* going to stay with Melinda.

'We'll give them five minutes,' Murray said.

Five minutes to lock the door, undress and jump into bed?

'You're very quiet,' Murray murmured when the time had passed.

'Aren't we supposed to be?'

'Hardly, out here,' he smiled, and checked the time again. 'OK, let's go.'

'Go where?'

'To check that they're safe.'

'You don't think anyone is waiting for them inside the apartment, do you?' Julia was out of the car in a flash, with Murray hard on her heels.

'Logically, no,' Murray said, running alongside her. 'But we have to check every possibility.'

They reached the plush gilt and glass entrance, and Murray signalled the porter to open the door for them. He did not do so, but slid back a small pane of glass to talk to them.

Murray held out an identity card, and the man examined it carefully, then opened the door.

'We'd like to know the number of Miss Harrison's apartment,' Murray said. 'She's the blonde who just came in with a man.'

The porter's eyes glowed with appreciation. 'She has 581 on the tenth floor.'

'Thanks,' Murray said, making for the elevator. 'Now we go gashle.'

'Gashle?' Julia was puzzled.

'Zulu for "slowly". I was there for six months.'

'I never knew you'd been to Africa.'

'In our game we go anywhere and everywhere.'

It was good to know, Julia thought. Maybe she would ask Murray to assign her to the Australian outback next time, or the Brazilian jungle. Anywhere, so long as she need never set eyes on Rees.

The elevator stopped on the tenth floor, and they made their way along the thickly carpeted corridor to 581, stopping directly in front of it for Murray to bend his ear to the door.

Julia heard the murmur of voices and, unwilling to eavesdrop, stepped back. But Murray had no such inhibition, and remained where he was, a slow smile creasing his face before he too finally stepped back.

'Everything seems OK,' he mouthed. 'Now, let's see where's the best place to keep watch.'

'We just passed an unnumbered door,' Julia said, making for it and finding it was a broom closet, dark and warm and smelling of disinfectant.

Murray came in with her and they left the door ajar, giving themselves a clear view of Melinda's apartment.

'We don't both have to stay,' Julia whispered.

'I'm enjoying myself,' Murray whispered back. 'It's not often I get to play "I-Spy".'

'You don't need to. I can manage perfectly well on my own.'

'Oh, sure. You just love being on duty twenty-four hours out of twenty-four.'

'It's what I've been doing for weeks,' she rejoined.

'I'm quite willing to send someone to relieve you,' Murray protested, moving closer to her and banging his shin against a bucket. 'Damn!' He rubbed his leg.

'Go home,' Julia said again.

'No way. *You* go home and get some beauty sleep.'

Fat chance she had of sleeping when all she would be doing was trying not to think of Rees and what *he* would be doing!

'I mean it,' Murray reiterated. 'Go.'

It was an order and she obeyed it.

Back in the apartment, she switched on the television to watch a late-night movie, but all she saw were Rees and Melinda in bed together, and she switched it off again. It was impossible to relax until Rees walked in. But, if he saw her sitting up like this, he'd think she was waiting up for him! Of course, she could always put on her broadest smile and say she'd had such a wonderful time she couldn't go to bed for thinking about it!

Then, amazingly—as if in answer to her prayers—he was in the doorway, smiling and clear-eyed.

'What are you doing up?' he asked.

'Thinking about tonight,' she smiled.

'*Last* night,' he said. 'It's after two.'

'Really? I'd no idea.'

'Had a good time?'

'Mmm, wonderful...'

'You'd better get some shut eye.' He turned away, yawning. 'I'm exhausted. See you at eight.'

As he disappeared, tears stung Julia's eyes. Exhausted, was he? No wonder! How many times had he and Melinda... She jumped up from the couch and rushing to her room, flung herself on the bed and burst into sobs, the sound muffled by her pillow. Damn Melinda and every woman Rees had been to bed with. But, most of all, damn Rees!

It seemed only a moment later that the sound of tapping brought her back to consciousness, and bleary-eyed, she sat up and squinted at her wrist-watch. Nine o'clock! As she swung her legs to the floor, Rees put his head around the door. He was fully dressed, bright and bushy-tailed, and she glared at him sourly.

Ignoring it, he gave her a wide grin. 'Good thing I'm your boss, or you'd be fired!' Only then did he take in her crumpled chiffon dress and mussed hair. 'Why are you still in your glad rags?'

'I must have flaked out.'

'I thought you didn't drink.'

'I wasn't drunk. I was tired.'

'That Mark must be quite a guy. Even *I* didn't manage to make you so exhausted.'

'Don't talk nonsense!'

But Rees was already on his way, calling over his shoulder that he would see her in the office.

Oh, God! That meant he'd be driving there on his own! Galvanised into action, she tore off her dress and dashed into the bathroom. What a sight she looked with mascara streaked down her cheeks and her black hair wild as a witch! But what did it matter in the face of Rees' safety?

Creaming the make-up off her face in one fell swoop, she donned panties and the first dress that came to hand, slipped into a pair of pumps—no time for stockings and bra—and tore out of the apartment, praying she'd find a cab was to hand.

She breathed a sigh of relief as one cruised past her as she reached the street, and, asking the cabby to drive as fast as he dared, she caught up with Rees' car as it turned down the ramp into the parking area of his office building.

Hardly had he stepped from his car when she was beside him.

'Good lord!' He was startled. 'Where did *you* spring from?'

'A gooseberry bush!' Eyes alert, she stuck close to him as they crossed to the elevator, breathing a sigh of relief as the doors closed behind them.

'Your face is shiny and still streaked,' he remarked conversationally.

Scarlet-cheeked, she rubbed at her skin with a tissue. 'That better?'

'Not much,' he grinned heartlessly. 'You look a real sight—for sore eyes!'

Her spirits rose. 'Do I really?'

He nodded. 'So does Melinda without make-up. Beats me why good-looking women want to plaster their faces with goo.'

Their arrival at their office saved her the necessity of replying, and he went directly into his room, where two senior engineers were waiting for him. It was noon before his meeting ended and she was able to go in to see him, feeling she owed him an apology.

'Sorry I overslept, Rees. It won't happen again.'

'Forget it. There's such a thing as *quid pro quo*, and you've worked late so often...' He leaned back in his chair, swivelling it gently from side to side.

Though his conference had gone on for nearly three hours, he showed no sign of fatigue. But then, he was a demon when it came to work. Only as her eyes met his did she realise he was studying her as closely as she him, a quizzical look on his face that she had never seen before.

'Lunching with the boyfriend, I see,' he murmured.

'What makes you say that?'

He waved a languid arm in her direction, and looking down she saw she was wearing one of her most expensive dresses, peach silk with a narrow pleated bodice and sunray pleated skirt. Heavens, she *must* have been in a hurry, to have picked this one out and not noticed!

'I just grabbed the first dress to hand,' she confessed.

'You didn't really think I'd fire you because you were late?' he said.

'Of course not, but——' She dared not explain why she had rushed, and changed the subject. 'What's on the agenda for this afternoon? Your diary's empty.'

'I'll be in the laboratory, then I'm going to our factory in Kent.'

Instantly she was alert. 'Who with?'

'Not Melinda,' he said gently. 'So stop glaring at me.'

'I wasn't glaring. Anyway, what do I care if you go out with Melinda—except that she's too nice for you?'

He laughed. 'Sweet Julia, always ready to cut me down to size. Didn't your mother tell you it doesn't always pay to be honest?'

'No.'

'Pity.' He rose and reached for his jacket from a nearby chair. 'You can have the afternoon off, if you like. I won't be needing you.'

'Are you going by car?' she asked as he went to the door.

'Helicopter.'

'May I come with you?'

'You don't need to accompany me *everywhere* I go.'

'As your assistant I——'

'Let *me* decide if I want you around.'

'I've never been in a helicopter,' she added, reverting to her little-girl voice.

Muttering beneath his breath, he nodded, and hiding her triumph Julia went with him.

Julia wasn't lying when she said she had never been in a helicopter, though she had flown many thousands of miles during her modelling career, and she was in no way prepared for the motion of this whirly-bird.

Although it was a warm summer's day, there was a strong southerly wind, and the helicopter bounced around the sky like a children's balloon in play. This motion, coupled with the appalling noise of the blades, made her decidedly queasy, a fact which Rees noted with malice.

'Serves you right,' he said as they landed and she stumbled out after him. 'Next time do as I tell you.'

She felt too nauseous to reply, and was glad Rees had elected to have lunch when they landed, rather than before, for her meal would assuredly have hit the ground before she did.

'Do—do you mind if I sit down for a moment?' she whispered, and, not waiting for his answer, sank on to the tarmac.

'You really *are* ill.' Bending over her, Rees took out his handkerchief and dabbed the sweat from her forehead and upper lip. 'Little fool. I bet you didn't even have breakfast.'

She nodded, still too nauseous to speak, and kept her eyes firmly closed so as not to see the ground still heaving around her.

She felt strong hands grip her as Rees lifted her to her feet, and then swung her up into his arms, cradling her effortlessly as he strode across the helicopter pad to the factory entrance.

Only when they reached the lobby did he set her on her feet. 'Lunch first, work later,' he said, as she went to thank him. 'And if you still feel queasy, go to the ladies' room and lie down. I'll be too busy to catch you before you hit the ground again!'

'I'll be perfectly all right when I've had a sandwich.'

And so she was, her natural good health returning once she had some food inside her. For the remainder of the afternoon she followed Rees around the factory floor. Security was naturally tight here, and there hadn't been any necessity for her to come, but something had impelled her, and she didn't wish to analyse it. Watching his camaraderie with the men, it was easy to see why he was well-liked, and she thought again what an unusual man he was: determinedly professional, and a determined playboy.

It was five o'clock before they took to the sky again—luckily windless—and six before they re-entered their apartment. No, not theirs, she reminded herself, *his*. Maybe eventually his and Melinda's, for there was no point kidding herself that the Australian girl would not be moving in with him.

'Seeing Melinda?' she asked casually.

'Yes. Seeing Mark?'

'Of course.' She saw a frown cross his face, and for a joyous moment she thought he was jealous, but his next words dissipated the notion.

'You're not seeing him on the rebound, are you?'

She was puzzled. 'Rebound?'

'From me. Not so long ago you loved me enough to want to marry me.'

'Oh, I've got over that,' she said airily. 'Once I discovered the type of man you were, I knew I'd never be happy with you.' She gave him her baby-eyed look, wondering what he'd do if she flung herself at his feet and told him she loved him. Why, he'd run so fast, his shoes would catch fire!

'I suppose you fancy yourself in love with Mark,' Rees muttered.

'It's funny you should say that,' Julia replied, 'because I——'

'Spare me your reasons,' Rees cut in. 'I'm picking Melinda up in an hour and I want to have a rest first.'

With Rees safely in his room, Julia contacted Murray. 'We seem to be playing the same record,' she apologised, 'but Rees is going out again tonight, and I'm not sure if I should follow him myself or see if you can put someone else on to him.'

'Neither,' Murray replied. 'Fact is, I was about to call you when you rang. The results of the enquiry into the plane crash was made public on the six o'clock news. It's been confirmed it was due to a wing-flap failure and had nothing to do with Rees' invention.'

Relief washed over Julia like a beach at high tide, and she almost cried with joy. 'So whoever has been threatening him knows they're wrong to blame him for the accident?'

'Hopefully. It's a man, by the way. Jack Ledbury. Only an hour before the cause of the crash was announced, the police managed to get to see him—his wife was one of the dead. Apparently he seemed very reasonable, but they're pretty sure he's the one who's been making the threatening calls. They didn't say so to him—merely that they were seeing *all* the relatives of the crash victims to put them in the picture as to the real cause of the accident.'

'So what happens now?'

'They've put a round-the-clock watch on him.'

'Does that mean my job's finished?' Julia asked.

'Not until we hear from Sir Andrew. But there's no need for you to guard Rees tonight.'

'What a relief,' Julia murmured. 'I'll catch up on my sleep.'

'Pity. I was going to suggest a quiet dinner together.'

'I had dinner with you last night.'

'That was in the course of duty. This would be in the course of pleasure.'

'May I take a rain check?'

'Absolutely.'

The call ended, and she ruefully wondered why she had fallen for the wrong man when the right one was available. She and Murray had so many things in common. They liked the outdoor life, they understood each other's work, and he was handsome and intelligent. In fact, it was a damned shame she was unable to fall in love with him to order!

Sliding a note under Rees' door to say she had a date, she took herself off to the cinema and, determined not to be home before he was, sat through the programme twice. Even then it was only eleven, and, tired from her lack of sleep the night before, she went back to the penthouse. There was no reason for Rees to know she had come back early. After all, he never came into her room to check up on her.

Stifling a yawn, she let herself into the mirrored hall, stopping in surprise as she heard the delicate strains of a Mozart concerto. She tiptoed towards her bedroom.

'That you, Julia?'

Damn! What finely tuned ears he had. 'Yes,' she said reluctantly, pausing by the doorway. He was sprawled on the couch and must have been there some time, for he was wearing the towelling robe she knew so well, and there was a stack of documents on the table beside him and a coffee percolator bubbling away.

'Care for a cup?' he asked.

Wanting to store up every possible memory of him—God, what a masochist she was!—she nodded and helped herself, then perched on an armchair near him.

'You're back early,' she commented.

'So are you.'

'I was tired, and Mark was very understanding.'

'What does he do?'

'Do?' She thought quickly. 'He has a—a nursery.'

'I thought that was women's work.'

'Chauvinist!' She stuck out her tongue at him. 'I mean he runs a flower nursery.'

Rees looked amused. 'Gardner by name and gardener by trade?'

She nodded, took another sip of coffee and studied Rees through her lashes.

He showed no signs of fatigue, but then, why should he? Making love to Melinda had probably refreshed him, and he had to be happy when he loved her so much.

'Melinda's a nice girl.' The words tumbled out of their own accord.

'Exceptionally so,' Rees agreed.

'How well do you know her?' Julia asked.

'Don't give me that,' he teased. 'You two didn't talk about the weather when I left you together last night.'

Julia accepted the rebuke. 'She said you'd been good friends and—and that she had wanted to marry you.'

He nodded. 'Melinda's always been honest about her feelings. In that respect she's rather like you. You're a very open person, too.'

Julia swallowed hard. 'I am?'

'Too honest sometimes. It's bad to wear your heart on your sleeve.'

'One can't help the way one's made.' What a platitude, but it was all she could think of to say.

'It's important you know the sort of person you are, Julia. If you do, you won't get hurt.'

'What sort of girl *am* I?'

'Sweet, innocent, surprisingly capable when you set your mind to it, yet obviously preferring a home, husband and children to a career.'

Fat lot he knew! Until his advent into her life, she had never even considered having a home, husband and children, and had believed that her work with Guardians was the most important thing in her life.

From the corner of her eye she saw him set down his cup of coffee and lean back on the sofa, his lids lowered, the dark lashes fanning his cheeks. Even in repose he exuded vitality and command, and she thought what a pity it was that his mother didn't know the person he had become. If she did, she would have to have a heart of stone not to regret her behaviour.

Julia longed to run over and fling herself into his arms, to feel the silken strands of his hair on her palms, touch her cheek to his lean one, rest her mouth on his.

'Sometimes people meet each other too soon,' Rees said into the silence. 'There's a wrong time and a right time, I guess.'

'And Melinda and you met at the wrong time?' Julia finished for him.

'Yes.'

But now Melinda had come back into his life, and the brooding expression on his face seemed to indicate it might be the right time for him. How ironic if everything she herself had said to him about a wasted life, a lonely old age, was giving him food for thought and reassessment. But life was full of ironies, and the most bitter one would be Melinda moving in with him again. If she did, there was no doubt that Rees would marry her.

CHAPTER ELEVEN

EXPECTING to leave Rees next day, Julia was dismayed when Murray called to say Jack Ledbury had given the police the slip.

'Looks as if he still blames Rees for the accident, regardless of what he said.'

'How could they have let him slip past them?' she exclaimed.

'That's what Sir Andrew's asking the Commissioner,' Murray said drily. 'Look, if it will make you feel easier, I'll bring someone in to help you. Ledbury's a desperate man and you've carried this assignment alone for too long.'

'Thanks for the vote of confidence,' Julia spoke equally drily. 'If my name were Julian would you be offering to send me a partner?'

'Your sex has nothing to do with it. But Rees needs more than one person covering him at a time like this.'

'Ledbury knows better than to try to take him in the office,' Julia said. 'Rees will only be vulnerable when he goes out.'

'Then let's hope he doesn't. He's been told the man's on the loose, so he may act sensibly and stay home. I double-checked the penthouse myself the other morning, and no one can force entry without blowing the electronic alarms installed there. Anyway, let me know Denton's plans. If he goes out with Melinda tonight, I'll send you a partner.'

As Murray hung up, Rees buzzed for her. He appeared completely unperturbed, and gave her a list of calls to make and appointments to arrange. She longed to ask how he felt about Ledbury's escaping through the police net, but, as she was not supposed to know, she dared not do so.

'Wake up!' Rees cut across her thoughts. 'I've been talking to you and you were miles away.'

'Sorry.' Hastily she continued making notes of the things he was asking her to do, and two pages were filled before he stopped. 'This will keep me busy all day,' she commented. 'You aren't going out, are you?'

'No, nanny, I'm not. I've some drawings to check and then I'll be in the laboratory.' He hesitated. 'There's something you might like to know. The findings on the enquiry into the plane crash have been published, and our grey box has been completely vindicated.'

She nodded. 'I heard it on the news this morning. You must be very delighted.'

His only answer was to lift his shoulders, and Julia almost shook him with rage. If he had any sense he'd stay right here in this office till Ledbury was found.

'That will be all, Julia,' Rees said. 'Take all calls and say I'm not to be disturbed.'

Nodding, she returned to her office. She followed Rees' instructions to the letter, and even when Melinda called apologetically explained he wasn't taking any calls.

'One of *those* days, is it?' the girl said sympathetically. 'When he surfaces, tell him I'll call him this evening.'

Julia gave Rees the message when he emerged from his office at lunch time, but he was so deep in thought that she didn't think he had heard, and she followed him down the corridor, careful to step behind a large potted plant—thank goodness there were dozens of them—whenever he looked as if he might stop and turn round.

Once she had satisfied herself he was in the laboratory, she went back to the office to make the rest of her calls, then returned to the laboratory to wait for Rees to emerge. It was boring hanging around for him, but far less boring than escorting a sheika to Harrods! At least here she was doing something worth while. Even so, she was glad when Rees finally emerged at five-thirty, and once again she shadowed him, only showing herself boldly when they were a few yards from his room.

'Are you following me?' he demanded.

'Can't a girl go to the powder-room?'

'Sorry. Guess I'm being paranoid. But everywhere I go you're underfoot.'

'Not for much longer,' she said brightly. 'I'm sure Mrs Williamson will soon be back.'

'What a relief,' he muttered, stalking past her.

She glared at his back, glad of a chance to dislike him, even though she knew it would not last.

Promptly at six he reappeared, jacket over his arm. 'Let's go home,' he said. 'I'm tired.'

Hiding her relief, she reached for her bag and they walked side by side to the elevator.

'Seeing the boyfriend?' he enquired.

'Mark isn't sure he'll be free, but—er—but I want to be available in case he is.'

'Don't make yourself too available, Julia. Men like to do the chasing.'

'Mark's chased me long enough,' she said demurely. 'I think it's time I let him catch me.'

Rees' eyes glittered. From annoyance that *he* hadn't caught her? Julia wondered. After all, it must be galling for a man used to success to suddenly have a failure.

The drive home seemed shorter than usual, and as Rees turned the nose of the car towards the underground parking she experienced a stab of fear.

'Leave the car on the street,' she said quickly.

'What for?'

'You may want to go out.' She said the first thing that came into her head.

'I'm staying in tonight.'

Her breath expelled in relief, though it was short-lived. 'I just remembered, Melinda called you earlier and said she'd speak to you at home. I'm afraid it slipped my mind.'

'No matter. I called her myself before I left the office.'

They drove into the vast area underneath the block, and Julia looked anxiously round, uncaring if Rees noticed, which of course he did. But, though his mouth thinned with annoyance, he made no comment. Luckily his parking bay was near the elevator, and she sent up a silent prayer of relief that it was waiting for them. Even before the ignition was switched off, she was out of the car, ready to shield him.

'Why the rush?' he asked as they entered the elevator.

'I don't like being underground. It gives me——'

'Claustrophobia,' he grinned. 'There are so many things you're scared of, I often wonder what *doesn't* bother you.'

Their arrival at the top floor saved her from answering, and she shot out fast and looked up and down the corridor. From the service elevator at the far end, a middle-aged man in a navy boiler-suit, tool box in his hand, emerged.

'Who's that?' she hissed.

Rees glanced at him casually. 'One of the maintenance staff.'

Knowing he was being watched, the man quickened his pace towards them. 'Just checking the lights in the corridors, sir.'

'That must take you a while,' Julia said.

'Nineteen minutes. Double that if any bulbs 'ave to be changed.'

Rees and Julia walked towards the penthouse door, the man pausing behind them to examine a switch.

Rees had his key in the lock when the man stepped behind them. 'I'd like to come in with you, if you don't mind.' The Cockney accent had gone, and the voice was quiet, cultured and menacing.

Julia's scalp prickled, her worst fears realised. How the hell had Jack Ledbury got into the building? Once the police knew he had left his house, surely they had put a round-the-clock guard on this block?

'You're making a mistake,' she said crisply, and went to swing around, only stopping as the business end of a gun dug into the small of her back.

'I'm not making a mistake,' came the answer.

'Haven't you heard the news?' Rees asked, still facing the door.

'Exonerating that marvellous invention of yours? Oh, yes, I heard it, but I'm not fool enough to believe it.'

'It's true.' Rees's voice was full of conviction, though quiet as the man's. 'The accident was due to wing-flap failure.'

'Don't give me that! We both know that grey box of yours will bring millions of revenue into this country, so it's only natural for the government to exonerate it.'

'It's not up to the government. The Civil Aviation Authority don't cover up the truth, and they're the ones who have issued the report.'

'Whitewash!' Jack Ledbury reiterated. 'Now, open the door carefully. One wrong move and this lovely young lady will get the first bullet.'

Rees did as he was told, and the three of them went into the entrance hall. The lights came on automatically, the domed ceiling above them glowing pink, the recessed lights in the walls casting a pearly radiance on the flowers standing on the circular, steel table in the centre of the floor.

In a few moments Rees might be dead. Julia found the thought unbearable. He was too full of vitality to die in such a pointless manner. He had so much to give, so much to live for. Yet tackling Jack Ledbury was out—his gun would go off before she even raised an arm—so she had to disarm him by catching him off guard.

'Please take your gun away from my back,' she begged in a pleading voice. '*I* haven't done you any harm.'

'You're Denton's girlfriend,' he snapped.

'I'm not. I'm his assistant.' She felt the gun ease away from her back, and very carefully turned.

Seeing Ledbury full-face, Julia's fears intensified. He was pale-faced yet calm, with a glow of determination about him that did not augur well for Rees' safety. She judged him to be in his early fifties—conservatively dressed, with pale brown hair and neat features. The sort of man you would pass in the street without noticing, or if you did, would think of as 'Mr Average'.

She wondered if she should mention his wife, then decided nothing ventured nothing gained. But she would lead up to it.

'What do you do?' she asked gently. 'When you're not waving that gun around, I mean?'

'I'm a civil servant. I was going to take early retirement next year, but your boss put paid to that.' The man's face clouded over, his expression no longer calm. 'Margaret and I were going to move to Cornwall. She loves—she loved the sea and... But all that's finished, and so is my life.'

'I'm sure Margaret wouldn't want you to say that.'

'How do *you* know?' Ledbury said bitterly. 'You never met her.'

'But she loved you, and if you love someone you want them to go on living.' Julia kept her voice gentle, remembering Murray stressing the importance of trying to establish a relationship with the person threatening you.

This meant encouraging them to talk, being sympathetic, putting on no pressure. Pressure. Yes, that was the danger, for it could make the knife flash, the finger pull back the trigger, remove the grenade pin. Easy now, she warned herself, easy.

'Was your wife a civil servant, too?' As she asked the question, she was aware of Rees staring at her as if she were off her head, but she was afraid to signal him with her eyes in case Jack Ledbury intercepted it.

'She gave up work when our baby was born. But Mandy died when she was three and Margaret never became pregnant again. I didn't mind, though. It drew us closer together.' Ignoring Julia, he looked directly at Rees. 'She was all I had and you took her away from me. That's why you're going to pay for it.'

'The grey box wasn't to blame,' Rees said firmly. 'It's as perfect as man can make it.'

'No more talk. You're a murderer and you're going to die.'

Julia, trained to sense the infinitesimal movement of muscles, felt, rather than saw Rees tense, as if, like an animal, he was girding himself to spring. But he would be shot before he got anywhere near Ledbury. No man, however quick off the mark, could beat the swiftness of a bullet.

Don't move, she willed him. Don't move. I love you, Rees, I love you.

'Killing Mr Denton won't bring Margaret back,' she said calmly, softly. 'And she wouldn't want you to have his death on your hands.'

'He's got *her* death on his hands!' Ledbury said with such anguish that Julia knew she had to act fast. Delay it a few seconds and Rees would spring—and be shot.

'Why don't we sit down and talk things over?' she said casually.

'Don't talk down to me!' The gun rose.

'I'm not! I understand how you feel.' Her voice was slow, slow, and soft as sigh. 'I really do understand.' Gently, she bent at the knees, twisted sideways in case Ledbury fired—and swooped across the floor in a rugby tackle that brought him crashing down, legs buckling, arms flailing. The gun went off in what seemed like an explosion, and the wall of mirror behind Rees shattered into a thousand scintillating pieces, like a waterfall. In that instant Rees was beside her, knocking the gun from Ledbury's hand and pinning him to the ground before giving him a sharp right to the jaw that rendered him unconscious.

Then he pulled her to her feet, his eyes blazing. 'What a damned stupid thing to do! You might have been killed.'

'And you'd *definitely* have been killed if you'd tackled him.'

'You're mad!' He shook her violently. 'Mad! Why the hell didn't you leave it to me?'

'Five seconds more and he'd have shot you.'

'How do you think I'd have felt if he'd shot you instead?' Rees shouted, still shaking her.

Wriggling from his grasp, she reached into her bag and took out a length of twine. Kneeling beside Ledbury, who was showing signs of coming round, she skilfully tied his feet together, then bound his hands behind his back.

As she did, she was aware of Rees dialling for the police, and when she straightened she found him staring at her as if she had grown another head. Which to him, of course, she *had*. A head that spelt 'bodyguard', a head that showed what a fool he had been!

'I don't believe it,' he muttered. 'You can't be . . . not *you*.' He glowered at her. 'Why the subterfuge? If you'd told me——'

'You refused to be guarded.'

'I see. So my estimable chairman took the decision himself.' Curving black brows lowered over glittering black eyes. 'I can understand him doing it, but to engage a woman!'

'They guard American presidents, too.'

'A woman,' Rees went on as if he had not heard her. 'Someone like *you*!'

'Why not *me*?' Julia demanded.

'Because you're a bundle of nerves. You don't like confined spaces, you can't bear heights, you hate...' His voice trailed away and he knuckled his forehead. 'It was all an act, wasn't it? Everything you said, your fears, your phobias, were all hogwash!'

'Yes.'

'But why?'

'To make you less suspicious of me.'

Only then did Rees smile, not a very pleasant smile, but one that was almost a sneer. 'You certainly played that part up to the hilt. I suppose all your talk about being turfed out of your apartment was——'

'A lie,' she admitted. 'The Sloane Street place is mine.'

'Did you say *anything* that was true?' he asked in an interested tone.

Only that I loved you, she thought. But I won't embarrass you by saying so. Anyway, you don't want commitment, and why should you, when Melinda has come back and is ready to live with you on *your* terms?

'Well?' Rees asked. 'You haven't answered my question.'

'I said and did only what was necessary for your safety. I'm sorry we had to bring emotions and personalities into it, but it was the only way I was able to be with you around the clock.'

'You're a marvellous actress, Julia.'

It was balm to her pride that he did not know she had ever spoken from the heart. Her eyes roamed over him, enjoying the broad shoulders, the narrow waist, the strongly muscled thighs. 'I'd better pack,' she murmured. 'There's no reason for me to stay here any longer.'

She was on the threshold of her room when he spoke again. 'I assume Mrs Williamson was in on the whole thing, too?'

'Yes.'

'So everybody knew about it except *me*? What a fool you must have thought me.'

'Don't be angry, Rees.'

'Angry that you saved my life? Or angry that you might have been killed by what you did?'

She was wondering how to answer this double-barrelled question, when he spoke again. 'You made a fool of me, Julia, and I deserved it. Sure I'm smarting at the moment, but give me a day or two, and I'll see the funny side of it.' The corner of his mouth twitched. 'Fact is, I'm beginning to see it already. If you——'

The rest of his sentence was cut short by the arrival of the police, and Julia was instantly the professional, giving them a report of the incident and watching with relief as Jack Ledbury was taken away. Only then did she go to her room and toss her clothes in her cases.

When she emerged into the hall, Rees was waiting for her. 'I'll take you home. It's the least I can do.' He hesitated, then came closer to her. Embarrassment was writ large upon him, and Julia knew he was remembering how hard he had tried to get her into his bed, and how she had played him for a fool over it. 'I realise that everything you said to me was part of the performance,' he muttered, 'but I'd like you to know that I—that I meant what *I* said to you.'

'That you wanted to make love to me?' Julia was amazed at how calm she sounded when she longed to hit out at him in fury and jealousy. 'Oh, I knew you meant that. It's the only thing you *do* mean when you talk to a woman!'

As if he hadn't heard her, his hand came out to touch her face, his fingers moving across her brow and down her cheek to linger a moment upon her lips. 'At one time you had me fooled you really loved me.'

'Sorry about that.' She forced a smile to her lips. 'I know the consternation it must have caused you!'

'But how cleverly you held me off.'

'Well, there are only certain things I'll do in the line of duty, Rees, and—er—you-know-what isn't one of them!'

He laughed and reached for her cases.

It was not until he had returned her to Sloane Street, deposited her luggage in her bedroom and bade her a grave goodbye, that Julia realised he had never asked her about 'Mark'. Heavens! He still didn't know 'Mark' was Murray Guardian, the man she worked for. Well, so much the better. If he believed she was in love with another man, he'd never guess her secret.

It was cold comfort, but it was all she had.

CHAPTER TWELVE

Two hours after saving Rees' life, Julia was facing up to the fact that her life was no longer her own.

For a girl who had always been fancy-free, it was chastening to admit that her happiness was dependent on a man who did not even know she existed other than as a beautiful girl he had tried to bed.

'I might as well have stayed a model for all the good it's done me,' she muttered as she stowed away her clothes and then stomped into the kitchen to see if there was food in the refrigerator. Predictably there was none, and she was on her way out to buy some when the telephone rang.

Was it Rees calling to say her departure had knocked him for a loop and he realised he loved her? She nearly tripped in her eagerness to lift the receiver before it stopped ringing, though her 'hello' dimmed to despondency as she heard Murray's voice.

'Why didn't you let me know you'd cornered Ledbury?' His anger reverberated in her ear, but it was no less than she deserved, though how could she tell him that misery at leaving Rees had pushed everything else from her mind? He would be furious with her for allowing personal feelings to interfere with her job, and part of her job was to let him know when her assignment was completed.

'I'm sorry, Murray. It slipped my mind.'

'What's wrong?' Always perceptive where his employees were concerned, Murray instantly heard the wobble in her voice.

'N—nothing. Reaction, I suppose. I'm fine, really.'

'You did a marvellous job,' he continued warmly. 'I'm proud of you.'

Knowing that if he continued in this vein, she would break down, she said brightly, 'All in a day's work, Murray. What's next on the agenda for me?'

'A week off.'

The thought of having nothing to do for seven days was intolerable, but even as she protested he cut her short.

'You've been working twenty-four hours out of twenty-four, Julia, and you owe it to your next client, whoever it may be, to be bright-eyed and bushy-tailed. Take yourself away for a week and enjoy yourself.'

'Very well. But if anything crops up for me before then——'

'A week off,' he reiterated. 'Don't you dare set foot in the office until then. 'Bye, Julia.'

'Murray, wait!' She was struck by a thought. 'Remember when I introduced you to Rees at Annabel's? Well, he doesn't know you're my boss. He still thinks you're my boyfriend.'

'You can always tell him the truth when you see him.'

'I doubt I'll bother. He's so busy with his own life, he couldn't care less about mine.'

'Then he's a fool. Forget him, my dear.'

Determined to try, Julia went home to her parents for the week. The moment she entered her rustic bedroom, built into the eaves of the lovely old farmhouse, her troubled spirits felt soothed. How good it was to be back, cocooned by happy childhood memories, warmed by her parents' love.

Her mother was quick to sense she was not happy, but did not impinge on her privacy by questioning her, and Julia, unwilling to talk of Rees—what was there to say beyond the fact that he had made a pass at her?—made a determined effort to put on a good face.

By the time she left for London, she was able to keep all thoughts of Rees at bay, except first thing in the morning and late at night, when the image of him, the memory of his voice, his touch, turned her limbs to water.

She drove straight to the Guardians office—having first checked that Murray would be there—and warmed to the sight of his breezy, blond looks.

'You look great.' He enveloped her in a bearhug before returning to his desk. He wasn't in his office clothes, but denims and a fine knit T-shirt, indicating he had just returned from, or was going to, the Guardian mansion.

In the event he had returned, having set up a new course for a fresh batch of recruits. 'I've got myself a partner,' he announced. 'He'll be supervising most of the training, and I'll go down for the last couple of days to test them.'

'I never imagined you delegating authority.'

'Blame it on age.' His face creased with humour. 'I'm thirty-eight, Julia. I want to ease up.'

'Poor old man,' she commiserated. 'Where's your bath-chair?'

'Not that old!' The way his eyes ranged over her gave meaning to his words. 'There's more to life than work, you know. Guardians is highly successful, I've plenty of money in the bank, and I'd like someone to share it with.'

'You won't have to advertise,' she smiled.

'Thanks,' he smiled back, his gaze lingering on her mouth.

Oh, no, Julia thought. Store detective work, here I come, for if Murray fancied her he'd start being protective, and once that happened it was goodbye to anything that smacked of danger.

'What's on your books for me?' she asked, as if unaware of the way he was staring at her.

'That sheika's back in town and——'

'No. Absolutely not.'

'Lord Burrows wants someone to watch over his daughter's wedding presents for ten days. You'd have to pretend to be a friend of the family, so you'll get a chance to wear your glad rags.'

'No,' she repeated. 'What else?'

'Bealeys want someone in their jewellery department for three months. They're doing some internal redesigning and they're worried about security.' Murray paused. 'No like either?'

'Afraid not. Come on, Murray. I'm sure you can do better than that.'

'Don't bank on it. Jobs like Denton's are few and far between.'

'Anything going abroad? There's been a spate of kidnap threats in France—surely that's put business your way.'

'Not so far.'

'Then it looks as if I'll have to go to one of your rivals.'

Murray pulled a face at her, then rubbed the side of chin, brow furrowed in thought. 'Look, I do have something that might suit you, but it means you going to Scotland.'

'As long as it's not guarding pheasants!'

He laughed. 'You might prefer them to the three children you'll be protecting.'

'Kidnap threat, eh?' Julia was vindicated.

'Yes. By a determined father. Their mother is equally determined not to give them up.'

'Why didn't you tell me about this job before?'

'Pure selfishness.' He rose and came round the side of the desk to stand beside her. He exuded strength, vitality and forcefulness, and she was sorry that his blond good looks did not make her heart beat any faster.

'Aren't you going to ask me what I mean?' Murray broke into her thoughts.

'No.'

Their eyes met, and in his she saw regret, ruefulness, and finally acceptance.

'Be ready to leave for Edinburgh in the morning,' he said crisply. 'You'll be met on arrival and taken to your destination. It's a few hours' drive from the city and somewhat isolated.'

Murray had not been joking when he had said the assignment was out in the wilds, for even though Julia had grown up in the country, this was more solitary than she had anticipated; a large castle, beautifully renovated and heated—the young châtelaine was an American heiress—and occupied now by her and her three rumbustious children: a boy of eight and twin girls of eleven.

Quickly Julia settled into a routine, and once she had established her authority over the children, who luckily liked her, she found it enjoyable looking after them.

The best thing about being here was that it was miles from Rees, so there was no possibility of bumping into him in a restaurant or nightclub. On the debit side, the many hours of solitude gave her too much time to think, and she was aware of a continual ache for him, a longing to hear his voice, breathe in the scent of him, touch him.

She knew that one day she would think of him without pain, but even when that time came she would never fall in love again with the same intensity. There was something special about Rees, not merely his looks, which were exceptional, but his strength of character and charisma. She wondered if Melinda would eventually succeed in changing his mind about marriage, and if they were already living together.

The idea of Melinda occupying the room she herself had used was to painful to think about. Then she knew how silly she was being. Rees, sensual man that he was, wouldn't let Melinda sleep down the corridor from him, when she could be in his bed and in his arms.

Only at this point did Julia succumb to tears, racking sobs that brought little relief. But a long while later, as she dried her eyes, she vowed never to cry for Rees again. He was gone from her life and she had to rebuild it without him.

CHAPTER THIRTEEN

JULIA had been at the castle four weeks when one of the maids came to tell her a man was waiting to see her in the library. Knowing it could only be Murray, and wondering if he was here to check the scene for himself, she hurried downstairs, having warned the children with dire consequences if they left the playroom.

The library was in the west wing, and she sped down endless corridors towards it, wondering how anyone enjoyed living in such a vast place, even though it *was* warm as a hothouse.

She opened the library door, her smile of welcome fading as she saw not Murray's rugged frame and blond hair, but the taut, lean figure of Rees. She opened her mouth to speak, but no words came, though he seemed unaware of it as he turned from the window to greet her.

'Hello, Julia. You're looking great.'

His voice was as deep as she remembered, his dark eyes just as bright. He might have stepped from the pages of *Men in Vogue*, so sartorially magnificent did he look in dark grey trousers and greyish tweed jacket, its cut superb, though the ensemble was clearly not new, which only served to add to its distinction. Trust Rees always to look perfect, she thought crossly, and was glad she was wearing one of her prettiest cottons, a soft lilac that deepened the lilac of her eyes.

'Fancy meeting you!' she said, her smile holding no trace of care. 'How did you know where to find me?'

'I rang the Guardian office. Some dragon of a woman refused to disclose your whereabouts, but when I explained who I was and why I wanted to see you, she gave me your address.'

Julia's heart raced. 'You came all the way up here to see me?'

'I had to come to Scotland, as it happens. I'm at Martlett House.' He named a mansion a few miles away that had been turned into a conference centre. 'It was a lucky coincidence, otherwise I'd have had to wait until you returned to London. But I wanted to give you this with my deepest appreciation.' From his pocket he withdrew a narrow, maroon leather box, and put it in her hand.

She opened it, lost for words when she saw a shimmering diamond bracelet. 'It's magnificent!' she gasped, 'but I——' she held it out to him '—I can't accept it, Rees. I did nothing to deserve it.'

'Except save my life. Or don't you think that has any value?'

'I didn't mean that.' She was distressed he had misinterpreted her. 'But it was—it was part of my job. Anyone else in my position would have done the same.'

'Maybe, maybe not. But you were extremely brave. Foolhardy,' he added, and clasped his hand around hers to press her fingers on to the leather box.

His touch burned her like fire, and she was intensely conscious of his nearness, so close to him that she saw the faintest dark shadow along his cheek, showing he had shaved very early that morning.

'Please accept the bracelet,' he persisted. 'It comes with my deepest thanks.'

Aware that to refuse again was ungrateful, she nodded.

'I'd like to see it on you,' he said softly, and, taking the bracelet from the box, clasped it round her wrist. His long fingers were deft, reminding her of how easily they had unzipped her dress and run over her body. Her cheeks burned at the memory and she lowered her eyes to the flashing fire around her wrist.

'I still feel it's wrong for me to accept this, Rees.' She forced herself to look up at him, a longer way than usual, for she was wearing flat sandals.

Noticing her tilt her head, he gave a lopsided grin. 'So the secret of your height was stiletto heels!'

'I'm five foot eight in my stockinged feet,' she flashed back. 'That's no midget.'

'It is when I'm six foot three.'

She moved away from him, saying carelessly, 'How's Melinda?'

'Fine. Busy filming that series of commercials she came over to do.'

'When is she going back to Sydney?' Julia waited tensely for the answer, remembering Melinda stating she wouldn't go if there was the slightest chance of getting back with Rees.

'She's remaining in London,' he said.

Julia's mouth went dry, and it was an effort for her to speak. 'You must be pleased. I know how *I* felt when—when Mark went away and then came back.'

'Ah, yes. Mark Gardner. Still on the horizon, is he?'

'Very much. He—he wants to marry me.'

'I shouldn't think he's the first one.'

'Nice of you to say so.' She edged to the door, yet for some reason could not leave. No, not *some* reason, she thought wildly, a very definite reason. She had to tell Rees that Mark was Murray Guardian, before he discovered it for himself. After all, Engineering 2000 might wish to employ Guardian Security again.

'There's something I'd like you to know, Rees. Mark Gardner isn't his real name. It's Murray Guardian.'

'Your boss?' Rees didn't hide his surprise.

'Yes. When I had to follow you and Melinda to Annabel's, I needed an escort, and he was the only man I could contact.'

'Then he isn't really your boyfriend?'

'He is *now*. That's the funny part of it.' Julia made herself smile. 'I'd always kept him at arm's length because he was my boss, and that night at Annabel's was the first time I'd let him take me out.' She paused. 'It made me see him differently, and—and I realised how I felt about him.'

Rees' mouth curved sardonically. 'I'm glad *some* good came out of this Ledbury affair. Are you going to marry him?'

'I'm thinking about it.'

One hand in the pocket of his jacket, Rees eyed her quizzically. 'I won't ask if all your talk about being an old-fashioned girl was true, or merely an act to hold me off!'

'I'm glad you won't ask, because I won't tell you,' she teased, and opened the door, afraid that if he didn't go soon she would fling herself into his arms and howl like a baby.

Together they walked into the main hall. 'I'll be here for a few days, Julia. If you're free at any time I'd be delighted to take you out.'

'I'm afraid I can't. I'm on duty round the clock.' She saw him to his car, filling him in on why she was here, and he looked so grim that she remembered his childhood had also been torn apart by divorce.

'You'd think parents would know better than use their children as bait,' he grated as he climbed into his Ferrari. 'I'd like to knock some sense into them.'

'I agree.' She stepped back from the car. 'Drive slowly, Rees. Country lanes are full of cattle!'

'I'll try to keep to seventy!'

'Do you good to use your will-power.' Only as the words popped out was Julia aware of their double meaning, and his laugh made her cheeks burn afresh.

'Still frank, I see.'

'Not usually,' she came back at him. 'That was the part I was playing.'

'And very well you played it, too. You certainly had me fooled.'

Thank goodness I did, she echoed silently, and remained where she was until he had driven out of sight.

'Who was that gorgeous hunk of man?' Cindy McAllen, mother of the three children, came out of the drawing-room as Julia closed the front door.

'Rees Denton. I did some work for his company.'

'Don't tell me you didn't fall for him!'

'I didn't,' Julia said abruptly, still fighting back the tears.

'I wasn't meaning to pry, Julia, but I—I guess I'm still a romantic at heart. Crazy, isn't it, when you think how badly Donald's behaved to me?'

Julia was not sure exactly what it was Donald McAllen had done, though gossip backstairs said they had quarrelled constantly. 'There's nothing wrong with being a romantic,' she said aloud. 'And you're still young enough to make another life for yourself, Mrs McAllen.'

'Except that I still love my husband, and I'll never feel the same about any other man.'

It was a statement Julia could endorse, and tears welled into her eyes. Mumbling that she had to be with the children, she hurried to the playroom, where eight-year-old Billy was laying into the eleven-year-old twins.

It was not until later that night, when she was locking the bracelet away and wishing it was as easy to lock away memories of Rees, that she allowed herself to think of him.

So Melinda was remaining in London. It confirmed what she had feared, and sounded the death knell to the faint hope that had foolishly lingered in her heart. Goodbye dreams, she thought sadly, and prepared herself to face a bleak future.

Julia had been at the castle two months when a black Jensen sneaked on to the estate and two burly men rushed from it and headed towards the children, who were cavorting on the tennis court.

Luckily one of the gamekeepers was with her, and while he headed off one man she brought the other one down with a karate chop, then alerted the local police on her walkie-talkie.

A chat to Murray later in the day brought another security guard to help her, but hardly had he settled in when Donald McAllen returned to the castle to talk to his wife, and a reconciliation took place.

Wishing all her cases ended as happily, Julia flew back to London and waited for another assignment. Only routine work was available, and throughout the autumn she was kept busy on unexciting jobs that did not tax her mentally or physically.

Engineering 2000 was in the news, for another major airline was installing the grey box in all their planes, and Julia switched on the television one evening and saw Rees being interviewed on a chat show, his usual incisiveness overlaid by a stunning display of charm which had the female interviewer drooling.

'How have you managed to stay single so long?' she asked coyly.

'At school, I won a gold medal for running.'

The audience roared their appreciation, but the interviewer persisted.

'Isn't there anyone special in your life?'

For an instant Rees looked serious. 'Yes, there is.'

'May we know who she is?'

Only then did the charm momentarily slip. 'Definitely not.'

Unable to bear any more, Julia flicked to another channel, then, bereft of his face, flicked back again. But the conversation was no longer personal, and she tuned out the sound and simply feasted her eyes on him.

It was a feast that gave her emotional indigestion, and she was awake most of the night, aching for him, tossing and turning with unassuaged desire, her breasts throbbing, her loins damp.

Predictably, in the morning she looked a wreck, but, model-girl training to the fore, she emerged into Sloane Street as beautiful as ever, though admittedly her make-up was heavier than usual.

She was between jobs, and she spent the morning shopping, buying a dress she did not need to cheer herself up, though it failed to do so, and debating whether to cut her hair short, which she finally decided against. And it was still only eleven o'clock in the morning!

With a sigh, she headed for the Guardian offices.

Since becoming aware of Murray's interest in her, she had studiously kept out of his way, but she felt so despondent that she decided to change her attitude and go out with any personable man who asked her—Murray included—in the hope that one day someone would ignite a spark in her.

This in mind, she walked jauntily into his office.

'Just the girl I wanted to see.' He rose and came towards her, holding out a photocopy of a letter. The words had been cut from a newspaper and crudely stuck on to a single sheet of cheap notepaper.

Carefully Julia read it. It was anonymous, and threatened the death of its recipient in the most ghoulish, cold-blooded manner.

'Whoever wrote this is a fiend!' she said flatly.

'Which is why we've been asked for one of our top operators.'

Miserable though she was, Julia rose to the challenge. 'Me?'

'You deserve it,' Murray said. 'But there's something you should know before you say yes, and if you decide to turn the job down, I'll understand.'

'Why should I turn it down?' Her eyes narrowed. 'You do want me to handle it, don't you?'

'Even if I didn't, I'd *have* to offer it to you. That's the basis on which...'

For the first time since Julia had known Murray, he was ill at ease, his fingers drumming on the side of the desk as he leaned against it, his eyes avoiding hers. 'The man who's received this death threat is Rees.'

'Oh, no!'

Murray nodded, his expression perturbed. 'He's specifically asked for *you*. He said he's used to you, and he doesn't want anyone strange.'

'What if I refuse?'

'Then he won't have anyone. He'll just take his chance.'

Her anger boiled over. He was still a fool, she thought stormily. 'It wouldn't be Ledbury again?'

'No. He's in a psychiatric hospital. We haven't a clue who wrote this letter. This is the third one, incidentally, and it's worried Denton enough to take notice of it. But as I said, you can refuse the assignment.'

'And leave him defenceless?'

'I'll try to talk him into accepting someone else. Ben's a good guy, and unobtrusive enough not to get under Denton's feet.'

Julia listened despairingly. Regardless of what Murray said, she knew he had no chance of getting Rees to change his mind, and that it was her or no one. But if she said no, and anything happened to him, she would be guilt-ridden for the rest of her life.

'Forget Ben,' she said quickly. '*I'll* do it.'

'Are you sure?'

'I don't have any choice.' Her voice broke and, hearing it, Murray swore under his breath and pulled her against his chest, his arms wrapping around her in a comforting hug. Julia's tears flowed faster, dampening his shirt, but he was uncaring of it and gently stroked her hair, holding her closer still, so that she was comforted by the warmth of his body, and the knowledge that someone understood how she felt and cared that she was unhappy.

'I wish you didn't still care for Rees,' he whispered against her hair. 'I'm much more suitable for you!'

She looked up at him with tear-drenched eyes. 'I'm so sorry, Murray.'

'Me, too,' he said with a lopsided grin. 'But that's the way the cookie crumbles.'

'It hasn't crumbled,' she whispered, 'it's fallen to pieces. He's in love with Melinda and she's staying on in London.' Her tears flowed faster than ever, and once again Murray drew her close.

'Darling, don't,' he said, then looked up startled as the door burst open and Rees strode in.

Julia, aware of steps behind her, moved quickly away from Murray, but kept her face averted, shaking with fear as she heard Rees' voice.

'Sorry to barge in on you,' he was saying in clipped tones, 'but I had a meeting with someone on the next floor and thought I'd drop in to see you.'

'If it's about employing me,' Julia swung round to face him, careful to keep her back to the light lest he saw the marks of her tears, 'then I'm free to start as of now.'

'That won't be necessary,' Rees said. 'That's why I came in. The letter was a hoax.'

'A hoax?' Murray questioned, his tall body leaning forward as if ready to spring. 'You're sure of that?'

'Quite sure.'

'How did you find out?'

'I have my ways, but the upshot is that I won't be requiring Julia's services.'

He regarded her again. The late summer sun streaming through the window deepened his tanned skin, giving added gloss to his shiny, black hair, and those wonderful dark brown eyes, marked by silky eyebrows. Yet it also showed new lines on his face, fine ones around his eyes, deeper ones either side of his mouth. Too many late nights, too much lovemaking, Julia thought bleakly, and glanced beseechingly at Murray who, reading her expression, came light-footed to her side. He did not put his arms around her—that would have been too obvious for Murray—but his very closeness, the protective slant of his body, spoke volumes, and Rees, glancing from one to the other, gave the faintest of smiles.

'Looks like I came in at an inappropriate moment. I'm sorry.'

'No need to be,' Murray said easily. 'Better you than one of my staff!'

Rees went to the door. 'I'll leave you to carry on where you left off!'

'Not in the office he won't,' Julia said, and kept a smile on her face until Rees had closed the door behind him. Only then did she collapse into the nearest chair. 'Thanks for saving my face, Murray.'

'Any time,' he shrugged. 'And now Rees is out of the way, we'll have to find something else for you to do.' He gave a mischievous grin. 'Hackenburg Junior needs to be escorted back to Texas. You do remember Hackenburg Junior, don't you?'

'His name is engraved on my heart!' She sighed. 'Is that store detective job still vacant?'

'Absolutely. For three months at least.'

'Then I'll take it.'

CHAPTER FOURTEEN

WORKING in a store was as boring as Julia had anticipated, and gave her too much time to think. Inevitably she was preoccupied with Rees, for, hard as she tried to forget him, he kept creeping into her mind, robbing her of appetite and putting shadows beneath her eyes and under her cheekbones.

The hazy days of autumn gave way to the crisper days of October, and Julia, walking home late one afternoon, succumbed to the blandishments of a flowerseller, and bought herself an armful of tawny-gold chrysanthemums.

She was arranging them in a vase when Melinda telephoned.

'You sound surprised,' the girl said.

'I am.'

'I was wondering if you're free this evening. I'd like to see you.'

About to plead a headache, an early night, any excuse she could find, curiosity got the better of her, and Julia heard herself agreeing.

'Shall we meet at my place?' Melinda suggested. 'I'm not the world's greatest cook, but I can rustle up an omelette.'

'Why not come here?' Julia suggested, unwilling to go to Dockside and pass Rees' home.

'Fine. I'll be with you about eight.'

In the months since Julia had seen her, Melinda had grown even lovelier. The less harsh British sunlight had made her hair darker, and it was now the colour of a golden guinea. The deeper hue intensified the big brown eyes flecked by gold, which gave her a slightly feline look. Yet she was a friendly feline, with no claws extended as she greeted Julia like a long-lost friend and helped prepare salad, while Julia set out a lavish cheeseboard.

'What a pretty place you have,' Melinda commented as they ate in the dining area of the lemon and white kitchen, and she glanced beyond it to the sitting-room, large and airy, its windows overlooking the green square where trees were already turning to russet.

'It's not bad for London,' Julia agreed. 'I suppose you've settled down completely?'

Melinda's mumble was unintelligible, and Julia let it pass, hoping the girl had not guessed she loved Rees and was trying to be tactful. The thought of being the object of pity was intolerable, and she was wondering how to get over it when Melinda spoke.

'I understand you saw Rees in Scotland?'

'Yes. I was on a job there and he was at a conference centre nearby.'

'Did you like the bracelet he bought you?'

Julia bit back a sigh. So Melinda knew. Not surprising, really. She had probably helped him choose it. 'It's lovely, but far too expensive a gift.'

'You saved his life.'

'All part of the Guardian service.' Julia smiled, and decided she had hedged long enough and would be blunt. After all, she knew what was going on and the sooner it was out in the open, the better for her peace of mind. 'How are things going between you and Rees?' she asked, popping a piece of tomato into her mouth and forcing herself to chew it.

'We're just good friends,' Melinda said drily. 'And I *do* mean friends.'

'I'm sure if you played your cards right...' Why am I telling her this? Julia asked herself angrily. The last thing I want is for Melinda to snare Rees. Yet maybe it would be better if she did. At least then there'd be an end to it.

'I don't *want* to have to play my cards right to get Rees to marry me,' Melinda admitted.

'Then bide your time and hope he'll see sense.'

'I'd live with him even if he didn't see sense! I told you when I first met you that I'd go back to him regardless.'

'Then where's the problem? You're here and he's here, and——'

'He doesn't want me.' Melinda saw Julia's sceptical expression. 'It's true. Randy Rees hasn't laid a finger on me since I came back from Australia, and that's more than four months.'

'You mean he fancies someone else?'

'Yes. Someone he's crazy about.'

'Hang in there,' Julia said sarcastically. 'With Rees's record, he's bound to fall out of love soon enough.'

The golden head gave an emphatic shake of disagreement. 'Not this time. You know what they say about playboys? They play themselves to a standstill, and when they finally fall, they don't recover.'

'Rees, faithful to *one* girl?' Julia scoffed. 'You must be joking.'

'I was never more serious in my life.' Melinda set down her fork. 'Tell me, Julia, how do *you* feel about him?'

'He's charming, intelligent, clever——'

'Are you in love with him?'

The unexpectedness of the question stopped Julia short, and colour burned in her face. 'Of course not.'

'Are you in love with Murray Guardian? Rees thinks you are.'

'I—er—yes.'

'And he loves you?'

'He wants to marry me, but I . . . well, it's a question of my career, and . . . you know how it is.'

'I think I do,' Melinda said bluntly. 'You're lying through your back teeth!' She leaned forward across the table. 'I have something interesting to tell you, Julia. You know those anonymous letters Rees was getting?'

'I certainly do. The one I saw was fiendish. If I knew who wrote it I'd——'

'It was Rees.'

Julia gaped. 'Did you say Rees?'

'None other.'

'But why?'

'To get you back into his life. He couldn't think of any other way.'

'If this is your idea of a joke . . .'

'It's no joke admitting that the man I love is in love with *you*. But I can't bear seeing him so unhappy. He works like a demon and I'm the only girl he sees. And only then because he knows I've accepted that he doesn't want *any* woman in his life if he can't have you.'

'You mean he's told you he loves me?' Julia found it too incredible to believe.

'Not in so many words,' Melinda admitted. 'You know how he hides his feelings, but I suspected it months ago, and this morning I found out for certain.'

'How?'

'Well, the other night I had dinner at his apartment, and the chain of my gold necklace snapped. It wasn't until I went to take it in to be mended this morning that I remembered I'd left it in his living-room. I rang him to ask if I could collect it and he said he'd put it in the top drawer of his desk. But it wasn't there, so I opened the next one and that's when I found the letters.'

'The letters?'

'And the glue and scissors and newspapers that he'd cut the words from. Plus the draft of the last letter he received—a letter he had written to himself!'

Julia was still disbelieving. 'Never! He wouldn't. He couldn't.'

'He could and he did.' Melinda reached for her bag, and from its capacious depths withdrew the draft of a letter and a newspaper article with numerous gaps in it where the words had been cut out. She held them under Julia's nose. 'There! See for yourself.'

Julia's heart started beating erratically. Melinda was right. This letter was a copy of the one Murray had shown her.

'Why would Rees do such a thing?' she asked.

'I've already told you. To get you back into his life. He went to Murray and said he didn't want anyone other than you to guard him. I guess he felt that if the two of you were together, he'd have another chance with you.'

'He soon changed his mind,' Julia said, her spirits plummeting as fast they had risen. 'Murray had just shown me the letter, and I'd agreed to take on the assignment, when Rees came in and said it wasn't necessary because he'd found out the whole thing was a hoax.'

'That's the only part I don't understand,' Melinda confessed. 'Why did he change his mind?'

'Does it matter?' Julia shrugged. 'It's more than two months ago.'

'It still matters to Rees. He's like a walking corpse. He loves you. I'm positive of that. So it beats me why he admitted the letters were a hoax.'

'Looks as if it will have to remain a mystery,' Julia said.

But Melinda would have none of it. 'When Rees told me he'd found out who had written those letters, he said you wouldn't have taken the job anyway, because you were going to marry Murray. Well, if he believed that, it was a good reason for him to abandon his plan.'

Julia cast her mind back to the scene in the office when Rees had arrived unannounced. She had just read that dreadful letter and had started to cry, and Murray had been holding her when Rees walked in. Was that why he had back-tracked on his mad scheme? Because he had seen her in Murray's arms and thought she had finally agreed to be his wife?

'What are you going to do?' Melinda enquired.

'I'm not sure. If Rees cares for me, why didn't he put up a fight?'

'I think he intended to—that's why he went to Scotland. There was no conference, you know. Mrs Williamson let drop that he was visiting a sick aunt!'

'Pity he wasn't honest with me,' Julia muttered.

'Were *you* honest with him? When you left him—after Ledbury was caught—you made it plain that everything you'd said to him had been part of your charade, so he naturally felt you didn't care for him.'

'What else could I have said when you were already on the scene?' Julia defended herself. 'I thought he was in love with *you*.'

'Rees *had* been carrying a torch for me,' Melinda confessed, 'but the night I came back from Australia and he took me out, he realised the battery was flat! Unfortunately you chose that same night to bring your boyfriend, "Mark Gardner" on the scene, and Rees saved face by pretending he still cared for me. But he went to Scotland to see you, and he did write himself those crazy letters, which was such a demented a thing to do, I can only think he's out of his mind with love!'

It was hard for Julia to credit this, for the Rees she knew was always in control of himself. Yet it sounded as if Melinda was right.

'If you *do* love him,' Melinda went on, 'tell him. Unless you're so proud you'd rather you both went on suffering.'

'You make me sound very stupid,' Julia murmured.

'People in love often are. Look at *me*. I'm still crazy about Rees, yet I'm handing him to you on a platter.'

Embarrassed, Julia swallowed hard. 'It's a generous thing to do.'

'I nearly didn't. I told myself if I hung around, I'd get him on the rebound. But then I realised I wouldn't be happy with him on those terms, knowing part of him would always be hankering for you.' Standing up, Melinda reached for her bag. 'Whatever you do, I wish you luck.'

'I don't know how to thank you.'

'Just make Rees happy.'

Alone again, Julia hesitated only for a moment, then dashed into the bedroom and searched out her prettiest, sexiest dress. With shaking hands she freshened her make-up and hair, then raced down to her car.

Not until she was outside Rees' apartment block, did she pause to wonder if he was in.

The porter, at his desk in the elegant foyer, recognised her as she peered through the glass door, and pressed the button to let her in. He had his hand on the intercom to tell Rees he had a visitor, when she stopped him, saying she wanted to surprise Mr Denton.

Succumbing to her brilliant smile, he nodded, and she winged her way up to the topmost floor, trying not to feel a sense of homecoming in case Melinda had got it all wrong. As she faced the black lacquered door with its shiny brass trim, she almost turned tail and fled. Then drawing a deep breath, she pressed the buzzer.

She was on the verge of pressing it again, when the door swung open, and she found herself confronting the man who, only a couple of hours before, she had hoped never to see again.

From the consternation on his face, he seemed to have harboured the same thoughts about her, and again she wondered if Melinda had got her wires crossed.

'Hello, Julia.' Rees' voice was formal. 'This is an unexpected visit.'

'I was passing by.' Only as she said it did she realise how silly this was. How could she be passing by the top floor that was home only to Rees? 'What I mean is I—I wanted to see you.'

He made no move to ask her in, and she stepped past him into the hall.

'I'd like a drink,' she said laconically.

'Sorry.' He sauntered ahead of her with the easy grace she remembered, and with economic movements began to pour out a fruit juice. Mid-flow, he stopped. 'I'm forgetting you aren't on duty. Would you like some wine?'

She hesitated, then said boldly, 'Champagne, please. I'm celebrating.'

He looked startled, then silently went out, returning after a moment with a bottle of Veuve Clicquot.

'Lucky I always keep one on ice,' he commented, opening it so skilfully that the only sound it made was as it bubbled into the narrow champagne flutes. 'As I don't know what we're celebrating, I'll leave the toast to you,' he said, raising his glass.

Julia could not take her eyes off him, mesmerised by his dark good looks. He was definitely thinner—Melinda was right about that—and paler too, which made his hair seem even blacker. She noticed it needed cutting, but decided it suited him longer, and felt her heart turn over as he raked it back with his fingers. He was dressed for an evening at home, his charcoal-grey trousers drawing attention to his lean hips, his matching silk sweater clinging to his wide shoulders.

'The bubbles are going flat,' he said, pointing to his glass. 'What's the toast, Julia?'

'To the man I love.' She raised her glass, then saw he wasn't doing the same. 'Drink up,' she said gaily. 'I don't think he's the easiest man, but he's the most intelligent, charming and sexy one I know. He's also blind, stupid and obstinate.'

'He sounds far from ideal,' Rees commented, still making no move to drink.

'You're right. But when you love someone, you love them warts and all.' Julia saw the tension in Rees' body by the way he gripped the stem of the glass, for his knuckles were white. 'Don't you know what I'm trying to say? Or are you really too obstinate to listen to your heart?'

Slowly Rees set down his glass on the table and moved closer to her, so close that she saw her reflection in his eyes. 'You've said so many things to me that you didn't mean, Julia,' his voice was deep and slurred, as if drunk with emotion, 'so many things that I'm afraid to believe any of them.'

'Well, you can believe this, Rees Denton.' She put down her glass too. 'I love you. I've loved you all along, but I wanted more than you were prepared to give at that time. But now I know you really care for me—thanks to Melinda—so I had to come and tell you how I felt.'

With a throaty murmur, he pulled her into his arms, gripping her tightly as he pressed feverish kisses over her face before finding the moistness of her mouth and draining it with the desperation of a man who had been wandering the Sahara for weeks.

Julia clung to him, giving him back kiss for kiss, moulding her body to his, exalting in the wild surge of passion that stiffened his thighs as her hands caressed his muscled back.

'Julia, Julia,' he said against her lips, an agony of longing in his voice as he drew her down on to the settee and his lap.

She curled against him, her breasts swelling to his touch. 'Unzip me,' she whispered, and he did so instantly, his face suffusing with tenderness as he took a pointed nipple into his mouth, his dark head heavy upon her shoulder.

Heat coursed through her, linking her breasts, her stomach, the throbbing bud between her thighs, and she arched against him in a frenzy of longing. 'I want you so much,' she cried. 'Oh, Rees, I love you, I love you.'

Slowly, as though with an effort, he lifted his mouth from her breast and held her away from him. 'And I love *you*,' he said thickly. 'More than I dreamed possible; more than life itself. I can't believe you're warm and real in my arms. The nights I've lain awake imagining this, aching for you, wanting to make you mine and never let you go.'

'You won't need to let me go. I'm here for as long as you want me.'

'For ever,' he muttered, straining her close to him.

Once again their mouths fused, and in an abandonment of desire Julia slid from his lap and lay back on the cushions, pulling him down on top of her. She revelled in the weight of him, the hardness of his thighs, the swell of his love, and twined her legs around his, vulnerable and open to him.

But he did not take her, and though his breath was heavy and his face had the sheen of sweat on it, he strained away from her. 'Not like this, Julia. What I feel for you is too... We must talk first. Why did you come here? You said something about Melinda, but I didn't follow you.'

Gently Julia told him of her meeting with the girl. She made it as succinct as possible, aware of his skin darkening with embarrassment as she referred to the threatening letters, though he made no effort to avoid her eyes.

'You can see what a fool love made of me,' he confessed when she finished speaking. 'I was so crazy about you, I was willing to do anything to give myself another chance with you.'

'All you had to do was say you loved me.'

'I believed you loved Murray!'

'And you let a rival stop you? I thought a knight fought for his lady.'

'I intended fighting for you—but subtly. Hence those letters I wrote to myself. Then when I walked into Murray's office and saw you in his arms . . .'

'It's a good thing Melinda came to see me,' Julia said sombrely, pulling him down to her. 'We've so much time to make up for, Rees.'

'I know.' His tongue feathered her mouth. 'These last months have been the most miserable of my life.' He nuzzled her ear, his hair silky against her cheek. 'I've still so much to learn about you.'

'After being with me for weeks?' she teased.

'You were playing a part then, and I still have no idea which is the real you.'

'The woman who loves you, who's willing to live with you on your own terms.'

Silently she vowed not to make the same mistake as Melinda and press for marriage, knowing that unless she compromised she would lose him. Maybe when he realised how happy he was with her, he would forget the unhappiness his mother had brought his father, and stop using her as a yardstick to judge all women. But she would say none of this to Rees—just make him as happy as she knew how. Show him that he was her world.

'You love your career, don't you?' he asked, deftly changing their positions on the settee, so they were lying side by side, and he could look more easily into her eyes.

'Very much. I find it interesting and challenging.'

'Dangerous too. I still wake up in a panic when I think how nearly Ledbury killed you. I've no right to lay down the law with you, Julia, but...' He paused for a long moment, then said firmly, 'If you go on taking the same kind of risks for your other clients that you took for me, I'll never know a minute's peace.'

Loving him as she did, Julia knew she would feel exactly the same if he was doing *her* job, and the admission showed her plainly what she had to do.

'I've no intention of risking my life, darling. In fact I've been considering going back to modelling. Then I'd at least be free to go abroad with you whenever you go. If you'd want me to, that is.'

'If I'd *want* you to?' He pressed her back on the settee. 'I want you with me all the time. I'll be miserable every minute we're apart.' His hands gripped her shoulders. 'I've no right to say this, but—dammit, Julia, do you think you could concentrate on me and give up modelling too?'

Before she could reply, he stopped her. 'No, forget I asked that. I know you enjoy working and... Dammit!' he muttered. 'I never thought I'd be so old-fashioned.'

'Old-fashioned?' She was puzzled.

'Old-fashioned enough to want us to live in the country, a place with a big garden, and dogs and cats and a horse or two.'

'You?' She laughed, her creamy throat swelling at the sound.

'Yes, me,' he said fiercely, his lips seeking the graceful curve. 'You've turned all my ideas on their heads. I've had plenty of time to think these last few months, and I've faced a few home truths about myself. I realised I was allowing the bitterness I felt towards my mother to colour my attitude to all women. Anyway, who am I to judge what went wrong with her marriage to my father? Sometimes it's difficult enough to judge one's own actions.' He paused, and when he spoke again his voice was barely audible. 'I went to see her a month ago. I doubt if we'll ever have a normal mother and son relationship, but at least I no longer feel bitter towards her.'

'Oh, darling, I'm so glad for you.' Julia could not stop the tears welling into her eyes, and Rees licked them away.

'About that house in the country,' he said. 'I'm happy to settle for a little weekend cottage.'

'I'm not letting you get out of your first suggestion,' she chided. 'I intend to give up work and concentrate on *you*.'

Delight suffused his face, and she glimpsed an unnatural glitter in his eyes. 'Don't let me talk you into anything you don't want, Julia.'

She wondered what he would say if she told him he had already done so, for in committing herself to live with him, knowing how adamant he was against marriage, she had forsworn her principles.

'I want *you*, Rees. Nothing is more important to me than being with you and loving you.'

'You won't get bored once the novelty wears off?'

'I might go back to painting. When I was sixteen I won a national portrait competition.'

'You're kidding!'

'I'm not. It was a pastel of our gardener's baby. I'm sure there's no shortage of babies in the country.'

'We can always make our own,' Rees whispered into her ear.

No, never, she thought sadly. Children needed the stability that came when a man and woman loved each other enough to make the commitment of marriage.

'Don't you want any?' Rees asked when she didn't answer, raising his head to look into her eyes. 'Or don't you trust me enough yet to marry me?'

'*Marry you?* But you hate marriage!'

'Not to you. I won't rest easy till you're tied and trussed.'

'As a liberated female I refuse to be tied and trussed.'

'How about adored and cherished, protected and sustained?'

'That'll do for starters.' With a cry of happiness she opened her mouth to him, and he drew her close and took what she offered. Her hands moved over his back, delighting in the feel of his muscles, the latent strength of him, the life-force he was longing to pour into her, yet was firmly holding in check.

'Make love to me, Rees. Make me yours.'

'No, Julia!' He jumped up fast. 'I can't. It's against all my principles. You have to make an honest man of me first.'

'I see. That's a pity.'

Straight-faced, Julia stood up and, as she did, her unzipped dress fell to the ground. She stood before him in the briefest of silk and lace panties and bra, and slowly she unhooked the bra and let it drop to the sofa. Then, resting a slender arm on a nearby chair, she stepped out of her panties. She felt her face go hot, but her lowered head, with its fall of silky black hair, hid it from his gaze, though her voice had the faintest tremble in it as she spoke.

'I don't know about you, Rees, but I'm too tired to go home. And as I've slept here safely so many times before, I'm sure you won't mind if I do so again.'

'Not at all.'

Leaving her clothes scattered around her, she sauntered gracefully out. The marble floor was cool to her feet, but she was burning with heat and hardly noticed it. She opened the door of the bedroom she had used, and saw it was exactly as she had left it, even to the paperback life story of Tom Cruise, whom she had pretended to have a crush on during her Bimbo act with Rees. She smiled at the memory, and sank gracefully on to the bed, running her hands lightly over the fine silk duvet cover.

There was a knock on the door.

'Who is it?' she asked languorously.

The door opened, and a tall, wide-shouldered man stood there, totally naked. His face was dark and shuttered, only the eyes—gleaming like jet, showed animation. A thin blue vein on his neck was prominent, as was the erratic beat of a pulse at the base of his throat, where a fine smattering of black hair dappled his chest, then almost vanished into a fine V lower down his body, but grew thicker again as it partially protected his manhood. A narrow waist merged into strong hips and then muscular legs, and these brought him to the side of the bed, where he stood, feet slightly apart, making no attempt to hide anything.

Pulse hammering in her throat, Julia regarded him gravely. 'Did you want to say something?'

He nodded. 'It isn't only a woman's privilege to change her mind.'

'I'm glad to hear it.'

'I thought you would be.' He knelt on the bed and bent over her, so close that the hairs on his chest rubbed erotically against her breasts, then lowered his body fully on to hers.

'Oh!' she gasped, and strained him close in her arms. 'Oh, Rees.'

'You talk too much!' he growled.

Her tongue licked his lower lip. 'So show me some action.'

Rees did.

INDULGE A LITTLE SWEEPSTAKES

OFFICIAL RULES

SWEEPSTAKES RULES AND REGULATIONS. NO PURCHASE NECESSARY.

1. NO PURCHASE NECESSARY. To enter complete the official entry form and return with the invoice in the envelope provided. Or you may enter by printing your name, complete address and your daytime phone number on a 3 x 5 piece of paper. Include with your entry the hand printed words "Indulge A Little Sweepstakes." Mail your entry to: Indulge A Little Sweepstakes, P.O. Box 1397, Buffalo, NY 14269-1397. No mechanically reproduced entries accepted. Not responsible for late, lost, misdirected mail, or printing errors.

2. Three winners, one per month (Sept. 30, 1989, October 31, 1989 and November 30, 1989), will be selected in random drawings. All entries received prior to the drawing date will be eligible for that month's prize. This sweepstakes is under the supervision of MARDEN-KANE, INC. an independent judging organization whose decisions are final and binding. Winners will be notified by telephone and may be required to execute an affidavit of eligibility and release which must be returned within 14 days, or an alternate winner will be selected.

3. Prizes: 1st Grand Prize (1) a trip for two to Disneyworld in Orlando, Florida. Trip includes round trip air transportation, hotel accommodations for seven days and six nights, plus up to $700 expense money (ARV $3,500). 2nd Grand Prize (1) a seven-night Chandris Caribbean Cruise for two includes transportation from nearest major airport, accommodations, meals plus up to $1,000 in expense money (ARV $4,300). 3rd Grand Prize (1) a ten-day Hawaiian holiday for two includes round trip air transportation for two, hotel accommodations, sightseeing, plus up to $1,200 in spending money (ARV $7,700). All trips subject to availability and must be taken as outlined on the entry form.

4. Sweepstakes open to residents of the U.S. and Canada 18 years or older except employees and the families of Torstar Corp., its affiliates, subsidiaries and Marden-Kane, Inc. and all other agencies and persons connected with conducting this sweepstakes. All Federal, State and local laws and regulations apply. Void wherever prohibited or restricted by law. Taxes, if any are the sole responsibility of the prize winners. Canadian winners will be required to answer a skill testing question. Winners consent to the use of their name, photograph and/or likeness for publicity purposes without additional compensation.

5. For a list of prize winners, send a stamped, self-addressed envelope to Indulge A Little Sweepstakes Winners, P.O. Box 701, Sayreville, NJ 08871.

 DL-SWPS

INDULGE A LITTLE SWEEPSTAKES

OFFICIAL RULES

SWEEPSTAKES RULES AND REGULATIONS. NO PURCHASE NECESSARY.

1. NO PURCHASE NECESSARY. To enter complete the official entry form and return with the invoice in the envelope provided. Or you may enter by printing your name, complete address and your daytime phone number on a 3 x 5 piece of paper. Include with your entry the hand printed words "Indulge A Little Sweepstakes." Mail your entry to: Indulge A Little Sweepstakes, P.O. Box 1397, Buffalo, NY 14269-1397. No mechanically reproduced entries accepted. Not responsible for late, lost, misdirected mail, or printing errors.

2. Three winners, one per month (Sept. 30, 1989, October 31, 1989 and November 30, 1989), will be selected in random drawings. All entries received prior to the drawing date will be eligible for that month's prize. This sweepstakes is under the supervision of MARDEN-KANE, INC. an independent judging organization whose decisions are final and binding. Winners will be notified by telephone and may be required to execute an affidavit of eligibility and release which must be returned within 14 days, or an alternate winner will be selected.

3. Prizes: 1st Grand Prize (1) a trip for two to Disneyworld in Orlando, Florida. Trip includes round trip air transportation, hotel accommodations for seven days and six nights, plus up to $700 expense money (ARV $3,500). 2nd Grand Prize (1) a seven-night Chandris Caribbean Cruise for two includes transportation from nearest major airport, accommodations, meals plus up to $1,000 in expense money (ARV $4,300). 3rd Grand Prize (1) a ten-day Hawaiian holiday for two includes round trip air transportation for two, hotel accommodations, sightseeing, plus up to $1,200 in spending money (ARV $7,700). All trips subject to availability and must be taken as outlined on the entry form.

4. Sweepstakes open to residents of the U.S. and Canada 18 years or older except employees and the families of Torstar Corp., its affiliates, subsidiaries and Marden-Kane, Inc. and all other agencies and persons connected with conducting this sweepstakes. All Federal, State and local laws and regulations apply. Void wherever prohibited or restricted by law. Taxes, if any are the sole responsibility of the prize winners. Canadian winners will be required to answer a skill testing question. Winners consent to the use of their name, photograph and/or likeness for publicity purposes without additional compensation.

5. For a list of prize winners, send a stamped, self-addressed envelope to Indulge A Little Sweepstakes Winners, P.O. Box 701, Sayreville, NJ 08871.

© 1989 HARLEQUIN ENTERPRISES LTD. DL-SWPS

INDULGE A LITTLE—WIN A LOT!

Summer of '89 Subscribers-Only Sweepstakes

OFFICIAL ENTRY FORM

This entry must be received by: October 31, 1989
This month's winner will be notified by: Nov. 7, 1989
Trip must be taken between: Dec. 7, 1989–April 7, 1990
(depending on sailing schedule)

YES, I want to win the Caribbean cruise vacation for two! I understand the prize includes round-trip airfare, a one-week cruise including private cabin and all meals, and a daily allowance as revealed on the "Wallet" scratch-off card.

Name ____________________

Address ____________________

City ________ State/Prov. ______ Zip/Postal Code ______

Daytime phone number ____________________
Area code

Return entries with invoice in envelope provided. Each book in this shipment has two entry coupons — and the more coupons you enter, the better your chances of winning!

DINDL-2

INDULGE A LITTLE—WIN A LOT!

Summer of '89 Subscribers-Only Sweepstakes

OFFICIAL ENTRY FORM

This entry must be received by: October 31, 1989
This month's winner will be notified by: Nov. 7, 1989
Trip must be taken between: Dec. 7, 1989–April 7, 1990
(depending on sailing schedule)

YES, I want to win the Caribbean cruise vacation for two! I understand the prize includes round-trip airfare, a one-week cruise including private cabin and all meals, and a daily allowance as revealed on the "Wallet" scratch-off card.

Name ____________________

Address ____________________

City ________ State/Prov. ______ Zip/Postal Code ______

Daytime phone number ____________________
Area code

Return entries with invoice in envelope provided. Each book in this shipment has two entry coupons — and the more coupons you enter, the better your chances of winning!

© 1989 HARLEQUIN ENTERPRISES LTD.

DINDL-2